The Uncouth Duke of Longford

HISTORICAL REGENCY ROMANCE NOVEL

Sally Forbes

Copyright © 2024 by Sally Forbes
All Rights Reserved.
This book may not be reproduced or transmitted in any form without the written permission of the publisher. In no way is it legal to reproduce, duplicate, or transmit any part of this document in either electronic means or in printed format. Recording of this publication is strictly prohibited and any storage of this document is not allowed unless with written permission from the publisher.

Table of Contents

Prologue 3
Chapter One 7
Chapter Two 17
Chapter Three 22
Chapter Four 32
Chapter Five 37
Chapter Six 44
Chapter Seven 50
Chapter Eight 56
Chapter Nine 63
Chapter Ten 72
Chapter Eleven 77
Chapter Twelve 87
Chapter Thirteen 93
Chapter Fourteen 102
Chapter Fifteen 107
Chapter Sixteen 114
Chapter Seventeen 122
Chapter Eighteen 129
Chapter Nineteen 137
Chapter Twenty 146
Chapter Twenty-One 152
Epilogue 158

Prologue

Bettina groaned and shook her head. "No, no, no! This is the wrong colour!"

"This is the colour you chose at the modiste and the yellow suits you very well," Rachel reminded her sister gently, though narrowly avoided being struck on the side of the head as her sister flung out her arms and then proceeded to stamp her foot very hard indeed.

"It is *not* the right colour! And it is certainly not the one that I chose at the modiste," Bettina declared, shooting Rachel a dark look. "Do not presume to tell me what it is that I have chosen and what I have done! I will not take kindly to it."

Rachel bit her tongue, knowing full well that the consequences of shooting a sharp response back to her sister would be rather painful. Bettina was the eldest of the two sisters and had always been domineering and arrogant though news that they were both to come to London and both to make their come out at the same time had made her even more so. Her mother, who was less than interested in either of her daughters and was much more interested in her own friends and the like, cared very little for how Bettina behaved. Instead, she left them both to sort matters out themselves, which usually left Rachel in a very unfavorable position – but what could be done about it?

"Rachel!" Bettina's sharp words forced Rachel's attention back towards her. "Will you answer me when I speak to you?"

"I am not one of the servants, Bettina." Making sure to keep her tone level – though she stepped back as she spoke to be out of the way of her sister's hands – Rachel lifted her chin a little, determined not to cow to her sister. "I am not forced to respond simply because you demand it."

Bettina's blue eyes narrowed, her face flushing red. "You are –"

"I am your sister and ought to be respected as such," Rachel replied, firmly.

"You are not worthy of my respect!" Bettina declared, angrily. "I see how you roll your eyes at me, how you complain and how you protest that *I* am much too difficult with my expectations and requirements. Do you think that *this* is how a sister ought to respond?"

Rachel's jaw tightened, her hands clasping together in front of her as she battled her anger. "Bettina, I would not do or say such things if you showed any sort of gratitude or sweetness of nature," she said, crisply. "I – "

She was stopped short by her sister's hand striking her hard across the face. Rachel stumbled back, one hand going to her cheek, shock mounting in her chest.

"Do not *dare* to speak to me like that!" Bettina screeched as Rachel rubbed hard at her cheek, tears coming into her eyes. "There is nothing wrong with my character, nothing lacking whatsoever! How could you think to say such things?"

Rachel opened her mouth to answer, only for there to come a scratch at the door. She called for the servant to enter at once, simply so that Bettina would be prevented from saying anything more. Her face stung still, her tears still threatening but she blinked them back furiously just as two maids came in.

"Your gown has arrived, Miss Grifford," the first maid said, dropping down into a curtsy. "Here. Should you like to try it on now?"

Rachel nodded. "Please, take it to my own bedchamber," she said, making for the door. "I will try it on there."

"That is a much better colour than mine."

Hearing the whine in Bettina's voice, Rachel turned her head at once. "This was my choice," she said, firmly, even though her face was still hot from her sister's slap. "My gown is a gentle green to match my eyes. There is barely any colour to it, to be truthful, and – "

"I want it."

Rachel blinked rapidly. "I beg your pardon?"

"I do not want my gown. You shall wear mine and I shall wear yours."

"No." Aware that Bettina would, no doubt, fly into a temper, perhaps strike her again and then complain to their mother if Rachel did not do as she asked, Rachel continued to stand firm. "No, Bettina, we shall not switch gowns."

"Yes, we shall." Bettina hurried forward, reaching out for Rachel's gown but Rachel quickly stepped in front of it, her gaze steady as she looked up at her sister who was half a head taller than she.

"It is *my* gown, Bettina."

"But I do not like mine," came the reply, "and therefore, I shall wear yours."

Rachel stood firm. "No. The yellow will not suit me. My hair is dark and my eyes are green, it will make me look sallow. That is why I chose the light green. Your eyes are dark and your hair lighter than mine. It will not suit you."

"I think I can make that judgement on my own," came the sharp reply. "Now remove yourself from my way and do as I ask."

Rachel held her sister's gaze, feeling her heart pounding furiously as she saw the steel flickering there. Bettina was going to get the gown regardless of what she herself did or said but all the same, Rachel could not bring herself to simply step aside and let Bettina do as she pleased.

"This is my gown," she said again, though with a good deal more firmness in her voice this time. "I will not step out of your way."

Bettina let out a shriek of frustration and, grabbing Rachel, shoved her bodily aside before hurrying for the door. Rachel stumbled, her upset growing as she heard her sister calling for their mother. Lady Carmichael who, unfortunately, always sought peace over fairness, would do whatever Bettina wished, simply so as to keep her sister placated.

"I shall not have opportunity to even try this on," she murmured, half to herself as the maids looked on, wide eyed. "There is little point." Sighing, she gestured to her sister's bedchamber. "Please, set the gown out onto my sister's bed. I have every expectation that it will be hers regardless of my own thoughts."

Just as she said this, another maid appeared at the door, quickly begging Rachel to go to speak with Lady Carmichael about an urgent matter. Sighing inwardly, Rachel nodded and then stepped out into the hallway in search of her mother.

Bettina had won again.

Chapter One

Rachel looked down at her yellow gown and let out a small sigh. Their mother had already decided that Bettina would be given whatever it was she wanted, and thus Rachel had been resigned – nay, forced to wear the yellow gown. It was their first ball of the London season, having made their presentation to the King the previous day, but unfortunately, she now looked pale and drawn. Bettina, on the other hand, looked absolutely beautiful in the light green gown which somehow suited her absolutely perfectly despite Rachel's previous protestations. It was unfortunate that the gown suited her so well, for Bettina had crowed over her success whilst Rachel had had no opportunity to make even the smallest murmur of complaint. Even if she had tried, she would have been silenced. On their way here, their father, the Viscount Carmichael, had made a comment on how pretty Bettina looked, while saying nothing to Rachel herself.

That had hurt. What had come thereafter, after their arrival at the ball, had pained her all the more.

"Good evening, Miss Grifford."

Rachel turned just to see a young lady smiling at her. She could not, however, recall the young lady's name though she did know her face, and the flush which came into her cheeks was one of embarrassment as she tried to smile. "Good evening." Forcing her smile to grow bigger, she gestured to the room around them. "Are you enjoying the ball this evening?"

"I am." The young lady's smile grew, her blue eyes twinkling with a sudden good humor. "Tel me, do you recall where we met?"

The smile on the lady's face was one which told Rachel that she had to be honest. "I am afraid I do not, for which I am highly ashamed and deeply apologetic," Rachel replied, her embarrassment sending prickling up her spine. "Goodness, you must think very poorly of me."

"Not in the least," the young lady replied, her eyes still twinkling. "There are so many people present and it can be hard to remember from one Season to the next!"

This remark made Rachel frown. "Though I have not been to any other season thus far."

The young lady's eyebrow lifted as she smiled. "Then can you recall where we met?"

Rachel chuckled. "Well, I do not think that we can have met in London, which means that we must have met at my father's estate or..."

"Or at my father's estate?" came the reply, and the young lady laughed, seeing the dawn of recognition on Rachel's expression. "Do you recall me now?"

Rachel nodded fervently. "Yes, I remember now! But of course, I am so very sorry that I forgot, Miss Renfrew. How delighted I am to see you again and especially here in London! I do recall that your father's house party was very enjoyable indeed."

The young lady laughed again, her red curls dancing this way and that as she shook her head. "Please do not apologise. It was a very enjoyable time and I am very glad that our friendship – which was only just beginning to blossom – can continue through the London Season." She looked all around Rachel before turning her gaze back towards her. "Might I ask where your sister is? I do hope she is present."

"Yes she is present, but she has gone with my mother and father to be introduced to one particular gentleman." Rachel watched at the confusion sparked in Miss Renfrew's eyes, no doubt wondering why Rachel had not been invited to go and be introduced to this gentleman also. She could not give an answer to an unasked question, for though Lady Carmichael had made it quite clear that Rachel was to remain exactly where she was – which was at the back of the room, hidden in the shadows – *why* she was not also to be introduced to this gentleman, Rachel had not understood. As she had stood there, watching the other guests at the ball, she had surmised that it was simply because her mother and father hoped there might be a glimmer of interest between this gentleman and Bettina. Clearly, Rachel might be considered a possible distraction so thus, this introduction did *not* require Rachel's presence in any way whatsoever. Bettina was to be the only noticeable person present, the only one worthy of any interest, and thus Rachel was to linger in the shadows.

That had brought a good deal of sadness to her heart but Rachel had attempted to force such feelings away. This was to be expected, she had told herself. Whatever Bettina required, Bettina would be given.

"I understand it is a little unusual for me to be standing here alone," she found herself saying, the pain beginning to grow within her heart all over again. "They are going to introduce my sister to this gentleman without my presence, though I do not understand why. However, I am sure it is for a good reason." She tried to laugh, but it came out a little brittle sound. "Whatever purpose my mother has, it will be to benefit my sister."

"I quite understand."

"Bettina is the eldest," Rachel replied softly, finding herself eager to give some sort of explanation, embarrassed to see the curiosity in Miss Renfrew's eyes. "It makes sense that she will be pushed forward."

"I am sure that is so," Miss Renfrew replied, her smile a little sympathetic. "But does that mean that you must stand here alone until they return?" One eyebrow arched. "Might you be permitted to walk around the room with me? As you may have noticed, I do not have a chaperone either."

Rachel's eyebrows lifted, surprise catching at her chest. "Goodness. No, I had not noticed."

"What say you, then?"

A happiness flooded Rachel's heart, pushing away her upset. "I suppose there could be no trouble in walking around the ballroom, no," she said slowly, thinking about how quickly her mother and father had dismissed her. The way her parents treated her with such disdain and disinterest made Rachel believe that neither of them would even notice that she was gone from where they had left her. Perhaps they would not even notice until the end of the ball! A wry smile tipped her lips as she nodded. "Yes, I think I shall. It will be a good deal better than standing here quietly!" So saying, she stepped forward and walked alongside Miss Renfrew as they began to make their way around the ballroom. All the same, they kept themselves to the side of the ballroom rather than walking near to where the dancing was taking place.

"Might I ask, Miss Renfrew, where your father is this evening? Is your mother not with you, rather than with him?"

It took Miss Renfrew a moment to answer. "My mother is with my sister who is presently nursing her first child."

"Oh, how wonderful."

"I thank you. It is good news." Miss Renfrew smiled warmly. "Therefore, my mother considered it a greater duty to be with my sister than to be with me, though my father did promise her that he would do the very best he could to secure me a match."

"I see." Rachel smiled and looked at her. "Is he nearby?"

Miss Renfrew's smile faded. "Unfortunately my father does not seem to believe that this promise to my mother requires him to be present with me when we are in a ballroom. He is, I think, in the games room, playing cards with various other gentlemen." She let out a laugh which to Rachel's ears did not sound in the least bit joyful or even a little mirthful. "Thus I am entirely by myself, though perhaps with you by my side, I will not look so improper. In truth, I did not know what I was to do with myself this evening."

"I am a little relieved to hear it for, in truth, I was feeling a little sorry for myself." Rachel shrugged lightly. "Mayhap we can be each other's chaperone – even though it is not exactly proper – but it is certainly better than standing alone." Seeing Miss Renfrew's smile grow all the more, she laughed lightly despite the sadness of her words. "I do not think that my own mother will care for my presence here at this ball, or at any ball. In fact, not until perhaps she has made certain that Bettina is married. Mayhap *then* I will be considered, though in truth, now that I say it, I do not expect that to happen, not even when Bettina is wed. Mayhap I will be thrown to some cousin or an ancient bachelor."

"Is that so?" Miss Renfrew looked back at Rachel, her eyes a little wide. "It seems that we are both in the very same situation, are we not? I fear that I too will be given an arrangement with anyone my father deems worthy."

Rachel sighed. "Yes, we are in the same situation, though I am all the more glad that you were willing to remain in my company even when I clearly had forgotten your name," she said, making Miss Renfrew laugh. "Now, you have been in London for one more Season than I. You must tell me which gentleman I am to avoid and which are quite suitable for me to stand up with, should I be asked."

"Oh, I am certain you *shall* be asked many times," Miss Renfrew said cheerfully, her smile big and bright. "But you are quite right to be cautious. There are many gentlemen here in London and a good deal of them have an attachment to their names which is not at all favorable."

"Then I certainly should be glad to know their names," Rachel replied quickly. "On our travel over here, Bettina was quite vocal, determined that she would have her dance card filled this evening, given that it is her debut ball. I confess that I am a good deal *less* inclined towards hurrying to that. I would rather be aware of the gentlemen and their reputations also. Not that I expect to make any sort of match this season, however." Her shoulders lifted and then fell. "But I can still dance."

"I am sorry that you will not be offered the same as your sister," Miss Renfrew replied softly, clearly seeing the pain on Rachel's face despite her attempts to hide it. "That is not at all fair, and my heart is filled with sympathy for you."

Rachel tried to laugh, tried to wave her concern away but she could not. Instead, she simply let out a slow breath and then shrugged her shoulders. "What is it that I can do?" she questioned quietly, aware of the heaviness in her soul. "It is not something that I am at all pleased with, but the situation is as it stands. Bettina will always be given preferential treatment and I am expected to bow to her demands also as though I was one of her servants! As though I was her lady's maid, ready to do all that is asked of me." Seeing Miss Renfrew's eyes flare wide with surprise, Rachel's face grew hot as embarrassment flooded her. Why had she spoken so? Why had she not been able to hold herself back? Flushing, she shook her head and then looked away. "Forgive me, I ought not to be speaking of such things."

"You carry a heavy burden. It is understandable that you would wish to have someone to speak with." Miss Renfrew looped her arm through Rachel's, offering her a small dose of comfort which Rachel grasped at once. "I should like to tell you something. Given that you have spoken to me with such honesty, permit me to do the same, that way, you will feel quite secure in the knowledge you have shared with me." There came a few quiet moments thereafter as Miss Renfrew's eyes grew serious and then shook her head. "I know what it is like to feel discarded. My mother does the very same to me, even though my sister is already married and, as I have said, given birth to her first child – a boy, of course – for which everyone is extremely delighted. My mother dotes upon my sister and is quite determined to spend as much time with her as she can. Even though this is my second season and there is a growing requirement for me to marry, my mother has no interest whatsoever in encouraging or helping me as I seek out a future husband. It is painful to be treated so. I can understand your pain, Miss Grifford, for I carry the same heaviness within my own soul."

Rachel nodded slowly, her heart filled with the sudden sympathy as she understood exactly what it was that her friend was talking about. How blessed she had been to come upon Miss Renfrew so soon after stepping into the ballroom! There was already a balm there for her painful heart. "Then we are very similar indeed," she said quietly. "I think that is a good thing, given that we will be able to understand one another and have the sympathy for each other's situations."

"I quite agree." After a moment, Miss Renfrew let out a quiet laugh, her eyes sparkling once more. "Did you know that I was standing a short distance away for some minutes and had watched your mother take her leave of you? I did think I would be a little odd to come over and introduce myself, but in the end I decided to do so. I am glad that I did."

"As am I."

They continued to amble around the ballroom, talking to each other and having no urgency to return to where they had come from or speak to any of the other guests present. At one time, Rachel caught sight of her mother and father as they stood together, talking to a tall, broad-shouldered gentleman, the one she herself was not permitted to be introduced to, but her attention was quickly diverted by her friend pointing out a gentleman Rachel ought *not* to meet. Everything was going very well indeed and, to her delight, Rachel found herself enjoying the ball a good deal, even though she was not dancing or conversing with anyone other than Miss Renfrew.

"Now, there is Lord Henderson."

Rachel listened closely to all that her new friend was telling her, seeing the various gentlemen and some ladies that were being pointed out. Lord Henderson, it seemed, was a gentleman who showed a great deal of interest in many ladies but never settled on anyone. He was a flirt and, to Miss Renfrew's mind, a bit of a rogue.

"I shall certainly make certain never to accept a dance from him, then," Rachel said, confidently. "I thank you for your guidance in this, Miss Renfrew. It is very helpful indeed."

Someone cleared their throat and Rachel started in surprise.

"Might you two ladies remove yourselves from my company? It is most displeasing to hear you speak badly about my friends and acquaintances."

Turned quickly, a gasp of surprise lodged in Rachel's throat as she stared into the face of a gentleman whom she did not know in the least. Quite why he had the audacity to speak so, Rachel could not understand for the gentleman ought not to be eavesdropping in the first place... though she would not dare to say so.

Thankfully, Miss Renfrew had no qualms whatsoever. "I beg your pardon?" Miss Renfrew's eyebrows arched, her voice rather loud. "I believe that I can say whatever it is I wish to *without* being interrupted by a gentleman who is not known to me.

"Is that so?"

Rachel took in the gentleman's face, seeing the way his lip curled and his dark eyes glittered with an obvious dislike as he sneered obviously at Miss Renfrew.

"You are speaking badly of those I call friends," he said curtly. "Either desist or remove yourself from standing near me. I do not like to hear such words."

Swallowing her friend, Rachel drew in a breath and spoke up. "Might I suggest that if *you* do not like to hear such words, you take yourself away from us, rather than expecting us to remove ourselves from you?" Rachel's heart clattered in her chest as the gentleman turned his eyes towards her, his gaze narrowing. Continuing to look at him steadily and lifting her chin just a little as though to prove to him she had no intention of acting upon his words, Rachel struggled to hold her gaze steady. The gentleman was sitting in a chair, his legs straight out, and crossed at the ankle and one elbow propping up his chin. His jaw was sharp, his eyes unwavering and dark hair scattered across his forehead. There did not seem to be even the smallest amount of happiness in his expression and Rachel resisted the desire to shiver lightly.

"You are both very impolite young ladies." The gentleman looked away, as though he could not bear to take another look at them. "It is just as well that you are standing near the back of the room. I am sure that no gentleman of my acquaintance would ever want to be in prolonged company with either of you."

His words stung and Rachel snatched in a breath, feeling tears burning behind her eyes. Miss Renfrew, however, folded her arms across her chest and held the gentleman's gaze steadily, her voice now rising with clear anger.

"And I believe that *you* are quite impertinent," she responded, though Rachel herself remain silent. "First of all, we see that you have been eavesdropping, and secondly, you place such a demand up on us that speaks of nothing more than arrogance. Indeed, I am quite astonished that a gentleman would demand such things of two ladies – two ladies whom he has never been introduced to! Pray tell me, do you speak to *all* young ladies in such a manner?"

Rachel found herself smiling, the heat behind her eyes gone as the gentleman frowned heavily. Miss Renfrew had a great deal of courage, Rachel thought silently, delighted that her friend had been able to speak with such terse words, forcing the gentleman to consider his own actions. That courage filled her own spirits and she nodded half to herself and in clear support of her friend's words.

Evidently, however, the gentleman did not take very kindly to Miss Renfrew's question, for he rose out of his chair and, coming closer, glared down at them both. He was a full head taller than Rachel and a head and a half taller than Miss Renfrew, making his stature rather intimidating. He clearly knew what he was doing given the way his eyes glittered, a smile carving its way across his face though it filled his expression with nothing but coldness. Miss Renfrew took a small step back but did not falter in her gaze, making the gentleman chuckle darkly.

"I do not think that either of you are aware of my title," he said, darkly. "You are entirely unaware of who it is you are speaking to with such sharp words and improper manner. If you did know who I was, then I am quite certain you would refrain in an instant."

"And yet, I do not care who you are or what your status is," Miss Renfrew replied just as quickly. "Any gentleman can still be a rude gentleman, whether he be a Baron or a Duke."

The firm way she spoke sent bolstering courage through Rachel, and she nodded fervently, refusing to let herself be cowed by this gentleman's rudeness. Miss Renfrew was quite right. Whether this man be a Duke or a Baron, or even if he was a knight, there was no need for him to speak with such disdain to either of them. What he was asking was entirely improper and would not be tolerated.

"It is not I who act improperly," came the immediate reply, this time his gaze turning towards Rachel and sending a cold shudder through her. "I hear you saying insulting things about various gentlemen and – "

"Miss Renfrew is speaking just as she finds, in order to protect me from any improper fellows," Rachel found herself saying as the gentleman's gaze swung back towards her again. "She is a dear friend and is treating me with great consideration. Simply because you do not like hearing what we have to say about your friends does not mean that you have any right to demand silence from us."

"Precisely."

Miss Renfrew beamed at Rachel and then looked back to the gentleman who had, by now, folded his arms over his chest and was looking away, his jaw working furiously. Evidently they had displeased him a great deal, but at this juncture Rachel herself did not care. No doubt she would have been quite terrified of this gentleman had she been alone, but Miss Renfrew's confidence added to her own.

"I do not think we need to linger here any longer, Miss Renfrew." Her voice was as loud as Miss Renfrew's had been, turning her head to look at her friend rather than at the angry gentleman before them. She offered her friend her arm and Miss Renfrew immediately looped hers through it. "I do not think that we will find any amiable company here."

With a giggle, Miss Renfrew turned and walked away with Rachel by her side, though Rachel could not help but glance over her shoulder to where the gentleman still stood looking after them. He was, she noticed, still gazing at them with a hard stare, his face a little red as his arms fell back to his sides. Rachel was quite sure she had displeased him, but she did not care. No gentleman should be permitted to speak to young ladies in such a way, and she herself was glad that the conversation had been brought to an end by them rather than by him. That showed him that they were not about to consider his views more important than their own.

"Do you have any notion as to who that gentleman was?"

Miss Renfrew shook her head. "Unfortunately, I do not."

"He did seem to state that he had a very high title," Rachel said softly, casting yet another gaze towards the gentleman, though he was no longer looking at them. "Not that such a thing matters, of course, for it is not as though my parents will be eager to introduce me to gentlemen such as he."

"My father does not care who I am introduced to. All he wishes is for me to make a match so that I will no longer be his responsibility." Miss Renfrew laughed rather than frowned, as Rachel had expected. "Though I certainly will never accept such a gentleman as that for a husband. Can you imagine what a sort of arrogance must surround him? He must constantly be talking of himself, thinking well of himself, expecting others to do just as he demands. I certainly would never tolerate a husband like that."

Rachel shivered at the very thought. Such a gentleman would do nothing but ignore his wife, she was sure. "He certainly was a bit of a beast."

"A *beastly* gentleman," Miss Renfrew laughed. "A very apt description, Miss Grifford."

"Rachel, please."

Miss Renfrew smiled. "Then you must call me Grace. After all, I am sure we are to be very dear friends."

"Yes," Rachel agreed quickly. "I think we shall be too."

Chapter Two

Andrew watched the two ladies for as long as he could before they disappeared into the crowd. He had not liked hearing them speak about Lord Henderson and others that he considered his friends. Though what had been said of them – particularly of Lord Henderson – was quite true, he would never admit that to them.

Such gentlemen were those he considered friends, though he did not go out into the ballroom in search of them. Instead, he chose to observe the ball rather than taking part in it. If he were to step out, then he would be surrounded by almost every young lady and her mother, all desperate for him to sign dance cards, eager to smile and tease and fluttered their eyelashes at him. Their attempts would, no doubt, come from a desire to make each of them appear a little more beautiful in his eyes than any other but Andrew had no intention of permitting *anyone* into his sphere. None, save for two or three particular friends whom he had known for many years. After everything that had happened, they were the only ones he trusted. He certainly could not bring any young lady into such a darkness.

Scowling, Andrew looked away, turning himself entirely in the opposite direction from where those two young ladies had walked. They had both been very rude indeed, he considered, for not only speaking such things to him but also for refusing his simple demand – and they had ignored him thereafter and turned to walk away, stating that he was not good company. His scowl grew. They had shown him such great disrespect as to suggest he was arrogant, selfish and had been eavesdropping, which was certainly *not* what he had been doing. It was not his fault that he had overheard them when *they* had chosen to stop so close to him.

"Perhaps they did not notice me," he muttered aloud, turning around to glance at the wall behind him. aware that he had hidden himself away. But all the same, he considered silently, they ought not to have been speaking in such a manner.

Silently, Andrew wondered why he had come to the ball in the first place. Yes, it was going to be full of debutantes, young ladies who had made their first foray into society, but such young ladies did not interest him. There were his friends, he supposed, which was something he could be grateful for. With a heavy sigh, he shook his head to himself, fully aware of his reason for being in London, though he did not truly want to admit it to himself. The only reason – the *main* reason – he had come to London was to escape from the heavy clouds which hung over his estate and lingered heavily upon his mind. Clouds which came from the questions which remained unanswered, the whispers which pursued him almost constantly.

His eyes caught on another familiar face and the heavy weight upon his heart lessened just a little. Lord Wrexham had been an impetus for his return, for he had written to Andrew on many occasions, practically demanding that he make his way back to society for the summer season. Given that Lord Wrexham was fully aware of all that troubled Andrew, the picture he had painted of society with its warm, welcoming joviality and laughter had tempted Andrew a great deal. Now that he had arrived, however, now that he was standing here in the ballroom itself seeing nothing but questioning eyes shot in his direction and looks of surprise shared between one person and the next, he began to wonder if coming to London had been a particularly wise idea.

"I have been absent from London for five years," Andrew reminded himself aloud. "It is to be expected that many will be surprised to see me present again." Seeing yet another lady look towards him and then turn to murmur to her friend, Andrew shook his head and sighed heavily. Being absent from London society had been both a choice and requirement. There had been so much to do at the estate, so much for him to learn and to take on, that he had not had a moment to think of leaving the manor house. With it had come a great many whispers about what had truly taken place over his father's death; questions which as yet, had still not been answered. His father's death had been unexpected and sudden and the manner of it suggested to Andrew- as well as to others - that it had not been of natural means. Andrew's only relief in all of this was that his mother had not been present at the time and did not know the true circumstances. Andrew had kept it from her and whether he would ever tell her the truth, he was not yet certain. His mother had been greatly distressed over the passing of her husband and it had taken her many years to recover. The last thing he wanted to do was to make her fall back into distress all over again. It was best for her to remain where she was with his sister, her husband and their children. That way, she still had some happiness and he Andrew alone would carry the burden.

"Do you intend to step out of the shadows this evening or are you planning to remain here for the entire duration of the ball?"

Andrew started in surprise, turning his head to see a gentleman grinning at him – a gentleman he had only just been thinking of. "Lord Wrexham."

"I have been observing you," his friend told him as Andrew scowled all over again. "Why is it that you insist on hiding here? Why must you hide yourself away rather than join in with other fine company?"

"I am not hiding myself away," Andrew replied, firmly. "I am merely observing."

"Which is watching rather than taking part," Lord Wrexham interjected, firmly. "Why do you not come and join me and the group of both gentlemen and ladies just over there? I am sure there would be many present who would be glad to see you."

Andrew shook his head.

"You are truly quite contented here?"

"For my first ball, yes," Andrew replied, quickly. "Do you not recall that I am a Duke? A Duke who has not been seen in some time?"

"Ah." Lord Wrexham tapped the side of his nose. "You are afraid that there will be those present who will immediately come to seek you out."

Andrew nodded. "I do. And I do not want company."

Lord Wrexham lifted his shoulders and then let them fall. "I am afraid that is going to be inevitable, Your Grace, regardless of when you should choose to make your presence known. In fact, I should say that the sooner you do such a thing, the better it will be."

"And yet, I am not convinced," Andrew replied, firmly. "Besides which, I have already heard two young ladies speaking in private conversation and, if that is the sort of creature which surrounds me here this evening, then I am all the lesser inclined towards doing what you suggest." His friend scoffed at this but Andrew kept his gaze steady and steadfast, refusing to be moved.

"You are still too much in darkness, my friend," Lord Wrexham said, sighing heavily. "Society is full of welcome and joy but yet, you persist in hiding yourself away. Tell me, have you not had enough of the shadows for a time?"

The question was spoken quietly but it made Andrew's skin prickle, anger beginning to flicker in his heart. "Be very careful, Wrexham."

"I do not mean to upset you *or* insult you," came the swift reply. "But you know very well what I am speaking of. This is not a time to carry those shadows forward. This is a time to release yourself from them, to fill your mind and your heart with strength which comes from friendship, from entertainment and the like."

Understanding what his friend was saying, seeing the kindness meant in his friend's words, Andrew took in a deep breath and then let it out very slowly indeed. "Forgive me. I did not mean to sound – "

"You have no need to apologise," Lord Wrexham interrupted, smiling. "I understand that this must be very difficult for you but that does not mean that I will not continue to encourage you. You will gain a very dark reputation if you do not."

"I do not know if I mind that particularly," Andrew replied, a little heavily. "Run along back to your friends and the curious young ladies who send me such inquisitive looks." He offered Lord Wrexham a wry smile as the gentleman looked over his shoulder and then back again to Andrew. "For the moment, I shall remain here."

Lord Wrexham let out a small sigh and then shrugged his shoulders, perhaps giving up in his attempts to help Andrew – for which Andrew was relieved. "Very well," he said, with another prolonged sigh which did nothing whatsoever to encourage Andrew to alter his present stance. "But you will come to Whites after the ball, will you not?"

Andrew shook his head and seeing the frustration on his friend's face, let out a small huff of irritation. Mayhap he was being overly harsh, mayhap he was being too quick to refuse Lord Wrexham but he could not bring himself to step out into the light, to join the ballroom, to smile at the young ladies and have them present their dance cards to him. Not yet, at least. It was too soon. He was not yet ready, not yet prepared for such a thing as that.

"The fashionable hour tomorrow, then?"

Hearing the hopeful tone in Lord Wrexham's voice, Andrew nodded slowly. "Very well. I will join you for the fashionable hour."

His friend grinned, though narrowed his eyes just a little. "I do not know if I can trust your word, Your Grace," he said, with a quiet chuckle. "Therefore, I shall come to call for you, I think. You may ride with me in my carriage and that way, I can make certain that you shall truly do as you have said."

Andrew opened his mouth to protest, opened his mouth to state that he had no need for his friend to chaperone him, only to close it again. Lord Wrexham was quite right. If he did not do such a thing, then there was every chance that he would change his mind, that he would *not* join him after all.

"Tomorrow, then." Lord Wrexham nodded and before Andrew could make even a single word of protest, turned around and made his way back to where the ladies and gentlemen were standing. Andrew scowled hard, disliking the fact that his friend had practically forced that situation upon him but finding that he could not make any real protest. This was why he had come to London, was it not? He had come so that he might find a little more enjoyment, that he might be free of all that weighed him down.

But the heaviness had not lessened. Indeed, to Andrew's mind, it seemed to have grown a little. It grew because of the realization that he could not be as so many other gentlemen were. He could not laugh and dance and smile as though everything were well with him, as though nothing else was of any concern. He could not even *think* of marrying, could not even imagine what it would be like to tell a young lady about the difficulties of his past. So what was left for him? Darkness? Lingering in the shadows in the hope of seeing even a flicker of light?

With a sigh, Andrew shook his head and stepped back so that the shadows wrapped around him a little more. *Perhaps I ought never to have come to London at all.*

Chapter Three

"Rachel?"

Rachel blinked, then pulled the sheet a little further up over her head. It was much too early for her to hear her sister's voice.

"Rachel!" The door cracked back against the wall and Rachel let out a groan, hearing her sister's footsteps bringing Bettina closer to her bed. "Get out of bed at once!"

"Why should I?" Rachel asked, keeping her eyes closed and the sheet over her head.

"Because I demand it."

Rachel let out a snort. "I do not give into demands, Bettina."

"Well, you should. This is vitally important to me!"

Rachel sighed heavily, her whole body still weary from the ball the previous evening. She had been asked to dance on three occasions – much to her mother's delight – and though she had danced them all without difficulty, she had found the whole experience to be utterly draining.

Bettina, evidently, had not.

"We are to be walking through the park for the fashionable hour today," Bettina declared, her voice echoing around Rachel's bedchamber. "I require your new gloves."

Rachel blinked, pushing the sleep from her eyes. "I beg your pardon?"

"I require your new gloves. I have just inspected mine and there is a slight error in one of the seams."

"That will not be noticeable," Rachel protested, pushing herself up to sitting. "I do not think that you require my gloves, Bettina."

"I do."

Rachel took in a deep breath and then lifted her chin. "You are not taking my gloves."

Bettina ignored this and began to rifle through Rachel's drawers, though Rachel, seeing this, pushed herself out of bed and hurried towards her sister.

"Stop." Closing the drawer quickly – and narrowly avoiding her sister's fingers – Rachel pushed herself in front of her and then folded her arms. "You are not going to take my gloves, Bettina. You have more than one pair of gloves of your own."

"But I have no *new* gloves," Bettina replied, sharply. "Therefore, I require your new gloves in place of mine."

"No."

Bettina lifted one eyebrow and stepped back. "I shall simply go to Mama and ask her."

"Go, then." Rachel did not move, fully aware that her sister might strike her again but even if she did, Rachel had no intention of removing herself from where she stood. Bettina might be more forceful, might have more determination than Rachel herself but Rachel had more inward strength. She was not about to permit her sister to demand yet something more from her even if it was a simple pair of gloves.

"You are being foolish, Rachel." Bettina's tone had become hard, her gaze cold. "My requirement is greater than yours."

"Is it?" Rachel lifted her chin a notch. "What requirement do you have that is greater than mine?"

Bettina's lip curled. "Did you not see the difference between you and me last evening? Did you not see that there were so many gentlemen seeking *me* out rather than you?"

The pain that struck Rachel's heart was great though she kept her expression as clear as she could. "That is because our parents decided that there were particular gentlemen which you ought to be introduced to rather than I, which is just as it ought to be," she said, firmly. "You are the eldest so therefore, you ought to wed first. That does not mean that there is any requirement for me to give you what is mine!"

"It is not as though anyone will notice what gloves you wear!" Bettina exploded, taking a step closer as though to forcibly push Rachel to one side and to look through the chest of drawers regardless. "*I*, however, will have many people looking both at and to me and I require those gloves!"

Rachel shook her head, her hands clasping tightly into fists. Bettina let out a scream of frustration and, after a few moments, turned and stomped out of the room, though the door was left wide open. Rachel heard the way her sister screamed for their mother and, instantly, turned so that she might find her new gloves.

"Miss Grifford, I must apologise."

Rachel glanced over her shoulder just as the maid brought in the breakfast tray, setting it down on the table by the fireplace. "I didn't know you were awake and – "

"Here." Rachel handed the maid her gloves, seeing the maid's eyes flare wide. "You must take these away. Hide them somewhere for me. I will require them later but my sister..." She caught herself before she spoke, instantly realizing that the maid – indeed, every single servant in the house – would know exactly what was going on regardless as to whether she said anything or not. "My sister is seeking my gloves for herself. I do not wish her to have them and so, I beg of you to hide them until I require them again."

The maid's eyes rounded. "I –"

"I trust you, Nelly," Rachel continued, hearing her sister's voice still echoing through the house. "Please, do as I ask and do it quickly."

Her lady's maid nodded, though her eyes were still wide. Reaching out, she took Rachel's gloves and then, after another glance towards Rachel, hurried from the room. Rachel let out a slow breath of relief and, picking up the tray, chose to return to her bed with it rather than sit in her night things by the fireplace. It was too warm for a morning fire but all the same, Rachel considered that the warmth of her bed was a little too appealing to be ignored. A self-satisfied smile spread across her face as she settled back against the cushions, knowing that at least in this, her sister was not about to have any success. She would *not* have Rachel's gloves, even if she wanted them and even if their mother demanded it from her, Rachel could simply say that she did not know where they were.

No doubt there would be consequences to her actions now. No doubt there would be a great deal of screaming and shouting and Rachel had every expectation that her mother would send for a new pair of gloves for Bettina rather than endure her fussing. *But,* she thought to herself, picking up her morning chocolate to drink, *she shall not have my gloves. This time, I have won.*

"My dear Rachel!"

Rachel smiled warmly as she caught sight of Miss Renfrew. "Good afternoon, Grace. How pleasant an afternoon it is!"

"Yes, very pleasant, though the park is going to become very crowded indeed, I think." Miss Renfrew made a face and Rachel laughed.

"I would have thought it would have delighted the *ton* to have so many present," she said, having never set foot out during the fashionable hour before. "But you do not seem to think it will be at all enjoyable."

Miss Renfrew shook her head. "It is a bustling affair! There are carriages everywhere, with many becoming trapped because they cannot go ahead and cannot go back. There will be many gentlemen on horses – sweaty horses, I might add – and there will be so many people present, it will be hard to distinguish one from another!"

"Goodness." The smile had faded from Rachel's face as Miss Renfrew had spoken. "I am surprised that Bettina showed so much eagerness in attending, then. She came into my bedchamber this morning in a flurry, demanding that I give her my gloves."

"Your gloves?"

Seeing her friend's confusion, Rachel managed a smile. "Yes, because my gloves had a perfect seam whereas hers did not."

"Oh." Miss Renfrew rolled her eyes and then giggled. "How foolish that is." Her eyes sharpened for a moment, her smile fading. "I presume that she did succeed in taking them, however?"

Rachel let a broad smile spread right across her face. "Ah, but I was wily enough to give my gloves to a maid so that she would *not* be able to demand them," she said, laughing at Miss Renfrew's surprised look. "She demanded them, I refused and thereafter, she went in search of our mother in order to make her requirements known to her. Given that my mother will always give in to whatever my sister demands, I had only a short while to come up with a plan to hide my gloves. I did so and then when my mother insisted that I give my gloves to Bettina since she is the eldest and, therefore, requires absolute perfection, I was able to say quite honestly, that I did not know where they were." She laughed again as Miss Renfrew giggled. "So my gloves are quite safe and therefore, I am quite contented."

"Though you are not wearing them?"

Rachel shrugged. "I did not think it a requirement to wear gloves this afternoon... at least, not my very best ones. My sister reminded me that every gentleman would be looking at her rather than at me so therefore, I chose an older pair of gloves instead." She said this lightly, her tone a little teasing but her friend did not smile. Instead, Miss Renfrew frowned heavily, lines forming between her eyebrows.

"That is not in the least bit true, however," Miss Renfrew stated, firmly. "There is no reason why a good many gentlemen might not look at you... even if you are not wearing your very best gloves."

Rachel laughed at this, making Miss Renfrew grin. She caught her mother glancing over her shoulder at her, perhaps a little irritated at the sound, perhaps thinking that Rachel was being a little too loud, but nothing was said and Rachel shrugged inwardly, looping one arm through Miss Renfrew's so they might walk together.

"Now, tell me," she said, quickly, "what gentlemen here should I avoid? After we were so rudely interrupted last evening, I should very much like to continue on with our conversation."

Miss Renfrew chuckled. "Oh yes, there are a good many gentlemen that I could point out to you, though I must confess that my interest has been piqued as regards the gentleman who spoke so rudely to us last evening."

"Oh?"

"I did speak to my father about him but my father had no knowledge as to whom I was speaking of." Miss Renfrew's smile slipped. "He was a little too interested in how many coins he had lost instead."

Rachel's lips twisted though she said nothing.

"I admit that I have wondered about him nonetheless," Miss Renfrew continued, her tone a little more cheerful now. "Mayhap we should ask Lord Henderson as to who he might be, given that he was the one we were speaking about when that gentleman interrupted us. Recall that he was displeased because he said that this gentleman was his friend?"

"I do not know Lord Henderson but would it not be a little strange if we simply asked him about this gentleman?" Rachel asked, frowning. "He would wonder as to why we were asking him, surely?"

Miss Renfrew considered this and then sighed. "I suppose so. However, I – oh!" She gasped aloud and came to a sudden stop, making Rachel stumble. A little confused, Rachel made to ask her friend what the trouble was, though Miss Renfrew's wide eyes and fixed stare had her quickly turning her attention straight ahead. She soon saw what – or who – it was that her friend stared at. The very gentleman she had been speaking about was standing directly opposite them, talking to two gentlemen and one lady.

Rachel's heart slammed hard against her chest, her eyes going wide with surprise. "Goodness, there he is!"

"Let us go at once!" Miss Renfrew exclaimed, making to go forward though Rachel held herself back, pulling her friend away from those intentions.

"No, wait a moment." Rachel found herself hesitating, wondering at that dark expression on the gentleman's face. "I do not think we should approach him. After all, he was not at all pleased with our company last evening and I highly doubt that he will want to speak with us again this afternoon."

Miss Renfrew smiled, her eyes twinkling. "Why should that matter?"

Rachel blinked. "I – I do not know. I do not want to irritate him." She bit her lip. Her instinct was to remain back, to hide herself away from this gentleman rather than approach him. Even though she was not of any particular interest to her mother or father, she did not want to bring any sort of embarrassment to herself and, therefore, to them.

"He will not say anything, if that is what you are concerned about." Miss Renfrew tugged her gently forward. "He is in company and with those that I am already acquainted with. Why should you be concerned?"

Rachel swallowed hard and though she paused still, her friend's urging forced her steps forward. The tightness in her throat dissipated as she drew in a little courage into herself, telling herself silently that there would be no difficulty in introducing themselves to the group. It was not as though they would be able to hide themselves away from the gentleman for the rest of the Season also, was it?

"Very well."

With a quiet exclamation of clear delight, Rachel permitted herself to be led forward, though she kept her gaze away from the gentleman as they approached the group. Miss Renfrew walked slowly, ambling almost as they drew near, only for her gaze to supposedly fall upon one of those present.

"Miss Hawthorn, good afternoon! And you also, Lord Bretford."

There came a flurry of welcome and Rachel forced a smile, though she did not look at the gentleman at all. Instead, she let her gaze rove lightly around the group, studiously avoiding him as she did so.

"Might I introduce you to my friend?" Miss Renfrew asked, before quickly making the introductions. Rachel smiled and curtsied, greeting first Miss Hawthorn and then Lord Bretford.

"And let me introduce you to my two new acquaintances," Miss Hawthorn said thereafter, gesturing to the two gentlemen that were left – which included the beastly gentleman.

"But of course!" Miss Renfrew exclaimed, turning to face them both, though Rachel's smile became a little fixed as she turned to look at them.

"This is the Earl of Wrexham," Miss Hawthorn said, as Rachel took in a tall, wiry, blue-eyed and fair haired gentleman who had a very generous smile and a softness about his eyes which endeared him to her at once. "Lord Wrexham, Miss Renfrew and Miss Grifford."

"A pleasure to be acquainted with you both."

Rachel smiled and dropped into a curtsy, though when she lifted her head, she saw with interest how Lord Wrexham's gaze now lingered upon Miss Renfrew.

"And the esteemed Duke of Longford," Miss Hawthorn finished, forcing Rachel's smile to disappear as she turned to the gentleman, barely able to look into his eyes. "Your Grace, Miss Renfrew and Miss Grifford."

"How good to make your acquaintance." The Duke's voice was low and gravelly, making Rachel's heart quicken as she dropped into a curtsy. Was he about to say something to them both? Tell the others gathered here exactly what it was he had overheard them saying about Lord Henderson? There was no truth in his voice, no obvious, expectant delight in his words. When he lifted his head from his bow, his expression was one pulled into a scowl, his eyebrows low over his dark brown eyes and his lips pressed into a sharp, flat line.

Rachel swallowed hard, struggling to look away despite the fact that only a few moments ago, she had to force her eyes to look into his. There was something about him that terrified her, she had to admit. Miss Renfrew's courage had emboldened her the previous evening but now, in this group of gentlemen and ladies, Rachel found herself quite afraid of him. It was as though all that he thought of her was written in his expression, and Rachel had every expectation of just how little she appeared to be in his eyes.

"It is very good to make your acquaintance," Miss Renfrew said, her voice filled with a warmth which surprised Rachel. "I do hope you enjoyed the ball last evening?"

"Oh!" Miss Hawthorn looked surprised. "I did not think you were acquainted already."

"We were not," Miss Renfrew replied, still smiling. "But we had occasion to talk, both Miss Grifford and myself, with His Grace, though we were not properly introduced."

"You were at the ball last evening?" Lord Bretford looked directly at the Duke, changing the focus from Rachel and Miss Renfrew and instead, returning it to the Duke himself. "I did not think that you were present."

Rachel finally dragged her gaze away, suddenly aware of just how clammy her hands had become. The Duke's presence was rather overwhelming and she silently wished she had listened to her own concerns and had remained behind and let Miss Renfrew step forward, had she truly wished to.

"Rachel?"

Rachel turned quickly, only to see Bettina and her mother approaching. She had not walked too far away from them, having stayed in sight of her mother though, given the look on her mother's face, it did not seem as though she was particularly pleased that Rachel had gone to speak with those that she was unacquainted with.

"Yes, Mama?" Rachel forced a smile as Bettina's lips quirked into a smirk, perhaps already aware of what difficulty Rachel was about to find herself in.

"Who is this that you are speaking with?" Lady Carmichael asked, her tone a little superior which made Rachel flush hot. "We are not acquainted with them and –"

"I have just made some new acquaintances, Mama," Rachel interrupted, speaking as loudly as she dared and ignoring Bettina's roll of her eyes. "Might I present my mother and my sister to you all? Lady Carmichael and Miss Bettina Grifford. Mama, this is the Duke of Longford, the Earl of Wrexham and –"

"The Duke of Longford?" Lady Carmichael interrupted, her eyes widening as she stared at the gentleman, her hand grasping Rachel's wrist in, perhaps, an attempt to silence her.

"As you see." The Duke's voice was hard, his eyes flicking from Rachel's mother to Rachel and back again.

"Why, I am acquainted with your dear mother!" Lady Carmichael exclaimed, surprise exploding through Rachel's chest. "I was truly sorry to hear of your late father's passing though I believe it was some years ago now?"

The Duke gave a small nod, though his expression did not change. "Yes, that is so."

"How very good it is to see you in London," Lady Carmichael continued, as the entire group continued to watch the conversation play out. "Is your dear mother present with you? I should very much like to see her again."

The Duke cleared his throat but shook his head. "No. She resides with my sister and her family at present."

Lady Carmichael visibly slumped. "I see. I shall write to her, however, and express my joy in seeing you returned to London. How glad I am that you are now acquainted with my daughter!"

Rachel heard this and for a moment, thought that her mother was referring to her given that Bettina had only just been introduced. She quickly realized that Lady Carmichael had put her hand on Bettina's shoulder and the two were now beaming at the Duke of Longford, leaving her behind them both just as they usually did. Her spirits sank and she closed her eyes briefly for a moment before turning her head away. Yet again, her mother had made it quite plain – both to her and now to those watching and listening – that Rachel was not worthy of the same attention as Bettina. Bettina was to be the one pressed forward, Bettina was the one who was to gain the attention first and foremost. Rachel was to get nothing.

"I believe I am acquainted with *both* your daughters now, Lady Carmichael."

Rachel's eyes flared in surprise as she turned her head to look at the Duke of Longford, though he was steadfastly not looking at her but held Lady Carmichael's gaze instead.

"Though I have forgotten your second daughter's name," he continued, as Bettina let out a squeak of embarrassment. "Forgive me. Might you remind me of it?"

Rachel blinked rapidly, her embarrassment beginning to fade as her mother hastily reintroduced Bettina again and reminded the Duke of Longford that she was not the second daughter but the first. At this, however, there came a dull, disinterested expression upon the Duke's face and though he nodded, he turned his head away and permitted the conversation to turn to something else.

Rachel did not know what to think of this though she found her heart almost a little delighted at his consideration of her. It might not be genuine consideration, she supposed, for it could be that he was simply being practical and wished to recall Bettina's name but, all the same, it had lifted her shame just a little. She looked to Miss Renfrew, seeing the same surprise reflected in her friend's eyes though she gave a small shrug as though to say that she did not understand the reason behind the Duke's remarks either. Letting out a small sigh, Rachel permitted a small smile to touch the corners of her mouth and as she lifted her head, found the Duke of Longford looking at her with those sharp, dark eyes. Her smile quickly faded and she pressed her lips tight together, unnerved by the scrutiny there.

He turned his head away thereafter and Rachel let out a long, slow breath and silently wondered just exactly who the Duke of Longford was... and how much of his true character he was hiding.

Chapter Four

Andrew shook his head to himself, scrunched up his paper and flung it into the fireplace. A note had come an hour earlier from Lady Carmichael, asking politely for where she might direct her letter to his mother and though he had responded – sending only the address rather than anything further – he had then felt rather guilty that he had not written to his own mother in some time. He had set to it at once though every time he did, every time he made to explain how he had been introduced to Lady Carmichael having already become acquainted with one of her daughters, he found his thoughts turning to the young lady and thereafter, his letter writing came to a sudden end.

It had been a very strange incident, he reflected, setting the quill down and choosing not to write for a time, in case that made matters easier. Lady Carmichael had stated how glad she was that he was now acquainted with her daughter but had not looked to Miss Rachel Grifford but rather to Miss Bettina Grifford, the one whose name he had pretended to have forgotten. He did not know why he had done such a thing as that – perhaps it had been the look on Miss Rachel Grifford's face when she realized what her mother had done – but he had first of all corrected Lady Carmichael that he had been introduced to both young ladies and thereafter, had pretended to forget the second young lady's name. Andrew could still see the shock which had written itself upon Lady Carmichael's face and the red dots which had struck Miss Bettina Grifford's expression, but he did not feel any regret for his deception. It had been very odd for the lady to ignore Miss Rachel Grifford, even though she was the daughter who had prepared the way for an introduction to him in the first place.

Though quite why I even noticed that and, thereafter, felt the need to say something to make Lady Carmichael aware of it, I do not know.

A knock came to the door and, a little relieved to be pulled out of his thoughts, Andrew acknowledged it with a call to enter. The butler came in and inclined his head. "Lord Wrexham, Your Grace."

A little surprised, Andrew rose from his chair just as his friend came in. "Good afternoon, Wrexham. Is there any particular reason that you have come to call?"

Lord Wrexham lifted an eyebrow. "Must there be a reason for my coming to call upon a friend?"

Andrew blinked, his face flushing a little. "Forgive me, I only meant –"

Lord Wrexham chuckled and waved a hand. "Have no fear. I am only jesting. Yes, I do have a reason to call, even though we are to see each other at the ball this evening." So saying, he sat down and then propped one leg up over the other, his ankle resting on his knee. "After yesterday's conversation in the park, *and* at the soiree last evening – "

"I barely spoke to anyone last evening!" Andrew interrupted, making Lord Wrexham's eyebrow lift.

"Yes, that is precisely my point," came the reply. "You are garnering a dark reputation and I am a little concerned about it."

Andrew frowned. "A dark reputation?"

"Yes. You appear sullen, ill-tempered and unwilling to make even the smallest effort to talk to anyone."

"I... I talked to Miss Grifford yesterday afternoon, at the park."

"For only a few minutes and I must say, even I was surprised at what you said to Lady Carmichael! Not that it was untrue but all the same, I do not think that it was required."

Andrew shrugged, having very little thought as to what other people thought of what he had said. "That does not mean that I am ill-tempered."

"All the same," Lord Wrexham said, a little more quietly, "you might consider what you are presenting to society. They have not seen you in London for some years and now when you return, you have a heaviness about you which pushes you back from people, which makes it appear as though you are entirely disinclined towards company."

"I am a little disinclined towards company," Andrew admitted, a slightly rueful smile at his lips. "There are some that I can tolerate, however."

Lord Wrexham let out a sigh – a sigh which told Andrew that he was not particularly enamored with the jovial remark. "All the same, I truly do think that you ought to consider society's view of you."

"For what purpose?"

"Because... because you will never be able to find a young lady to marry you if you do not."

Andrew immediately let out a snort. "But you know very well that I have no interest in marrying."

"And yet, you shall have to one day."

With a slight shrug, Andrew looked away. "I will arrange a marriage when the time comes.

"I do not require you to tell me what it is that I ought to do." Andrew's scowl began to pull at his features, only for his friend's eyebrows to lift, reminding Andrew silently of all that had just been said about his demeanor and the like. "I appreciate your concern," he continued, a little more quietly now. "But please, do not try to tell me what I ought to do. After the heavy darkness of living in my estate, knowing what I do, I would prefer no young lady be brought into that."

"You are speaking of the death of your father."

Andrew nodded. "You are one of the few people who know of my thoughts as to what happened."

Lord Wrexham's expression grew very heavy indeed, a shadow passing across his expression. "Your brother knows of it?"

Andrew shook his head. "I have told yourself, Lord Henderson and my cousin."

"Your cousin?"

Andrew nodded. "Lord Chiddick. Are you acquainted with him?"

"Ah." A flicker of recognition came into Lord Wrexham's face. "Yes, I do know of whom you speak. He is in Bath at present, I believe."

"I do not know. The truth is, I did not mean to speak to my cousin about my thoughts as regards my father's passing but on the day of the funeral – and after I had imbibed a little too much – I found myself speaking of it with a great deal of liberty. I regret doing so a great deal, I assure you."

"You told him that you believed your father's riding accident was not, in fact, an accident?"

Andrew nodded. "I did. I told him about what I found in the woods." His shoulders dropped, recalling how he had discovered a red bit of cloth very close to where his father's horse had reared up in fright, dropping him from the horse. That red bit of cloth had been tied to a stick, making him believe that someone had stepped out with it suddenly, frightening the horse and leading to his father's untimely death.

"Do you remember what he said?"

Andrew sighed. "Not all of it and certainly not clearly. What I do recall is that he said there was nothing that could be done, that I was going to be quite unable to prove anything and therefore, to his mind, I ought to give up the whole notion and concentrate on my responsibilities."

Lord Wrexham considered this, then nodded slowly. "I suppose that is true. What can you do about it? Even if you have your suspicions, even if you believe that your father's death was brought about by another's hand, then what can you do to prove it? What can you do to discover that person? Lord Chiddick is right to state that your responsibilities must come first."

Andrew sighed heavily. "Which I have done," he admitted, "though my thoughts as regards my father have never ceased. I do not know what it is I am to do about such a troubling thought but it lingers there nonetheless."

"And you do not wish to bring in a young lady to your manor house – to your life – when you have such questions?"

Considering this, Andrew shook his head. "No, I do not. After all, I do not know what it was that made this person eager to remove my father from this earth and, in truth, I am a little concerned that should someone else reside in my manor house with me, they might be in danger."

Lord Wrexham's eyebrows shot upwards. "In danger?"

"Yes."

His friend swallowed hard, his eyes a little rounder than before. "You believe that there could be someone eager to pursue your death also?"

"I do not know but it is surely a possibility," Andrew answered, truthfully. "Though it could also be that my father had some enemy that I was unaware of and that is the reason for his death."

"Or it could be a mere accident," Lord Wrexham put in, making Andrew sigh and look away. "That is also surely a possibility."

Spreading his hands, Andrew looked back at his friend. "Regardless, I will still be cautious and careful and until my mind is at ease, until I am satisfied, I will not bring in a young lady into my home."

"And if you are never satisfied?"

Andrew bunched his mouth for a moment and then let his hands drop to his knees. "I will consider that at a later time," he stated, firmly. "For the moment, I will do what I can to enjoy society while, at the same time, being quite intentional about those I bring into my sphere."

Lord Wrexham let out a long, slow breath and then shook his head. "And you will not care if society thinks you a dark, ill-tempered fellow?"

"No," Andrew stated, firmly. "I will not care in the least."

Chapter Five

"I do hope the Duke of Longford will be present this evening!"

Rachel attempted to keep her expression clear of any sort of wryness, turning her head away and smoothing her gown with long, gentle strokes though it did not have even the smallest crease in it whatsoever.

"I think you made quite the impression upon him in the park, Bettina," Lady Carmichael exclaimed, as Rachel dropped her head even lower, making sure that neither her mother nor her sister could see her expression. "Though I must say, I did find his manner a little... dark."

Rachel lifted her head to see her mother frowning, though Bettina was finishing pulling on her gloves as they waited for their carriage to arrive. She had to admit that the Duke of Longford *had* been very unorthodox in the way he had corrected their mother and even now, she could still feel that ripple of surprise rushing up her spine as she took in what he had said to her mother.

"I did not find *that* particularly pleasing, I must admit," Bettina said, her voice turning into something of a whine. "He had no reason to correct you, Mama. I am sure that he was well able to understand your meaning."

"There is a heaviness about his expression and his demeanour," Lady Carmichael admitted, quietly. "I must confess that is something of a concern – though I should still like you to be in his company as often as you can this evening, Bettina. It may be that your presence will lift his heavy spirits."

"I should like that," Bettina sighed, sounding quite contented. "I am sure that I will be able to make him laugh and smile and the like. All I require is an opportunity to be in his company."

"Which you will be sure to have," Lady Carmichael said, determinedly. "Ah, there is our carriage. Come now, Bettina."

Rachel's heart dropped as her mother gestured for Bettina to step forward, leaving Rachel herself to trail behind. Yet again, she was being forgotten about. Yet again, she was left entirely alone and if she had remained behind, if she had chosen to stay at home, Rachel was quite certain that her mother would not even have noticed her absence.

Sitting down in the carriage seat, Rachel folded her hands in her lap and looked out of the window. The streets were dark, the moon already high in the sky though the sky itself was not overly black thanks to the summer hours. She let out a slow breath of relief, her smile lifting gently as she took in the beauty of the evening. Even in this moment, even in the way that her mother forgot about her, she could still have a little happiness. There was still beauty here and, she had to hope that Miss Renfrew would be present as well this evening, so she might have a little company.

She did not have to wait for long to see that she had been right to hope. Miss Renfrew was waiting for her when she walked into the ballroom and immediately slung her arm through Rachel's.

"How glad I am to see you! My father deposited me with a friend and thereafter, took himself to the games room so he might play cards with another gentleman."

"I am sorry to hear it." Rachel offered her friend a small smile. "I have not yet been introduced to your father."

"I shall do so at the very next opportunity," Miss Renfrew promised, "though I cannot say when that will be, I am afraid."

Rachel smiled back at her and then, glancing to where her mother had begun to walk Bettina in one direction, turned them both in the same direction also. "I should follow, though it seems as though my father has gone in the same direction as yours, given that he is now nowhere to be found!"

Miss Renfrew chuckled quietly. "Would wish that I was a gentleman! I would be able to go where I pleased and do whatever I wished without any concerns whatsoever. Though I am not certain I should enjoy gambling in the same way that my father appears to! It takes up almost all of his time and indeed, he does not do anything other than this with his companions. That and drink a good deal of port or French brandy!"

Rachel laughed at this, her spirits lifting all the more. Even though the circumstances were a little less than delightful, she found herself happy that her friend was present. "Now, do you think that you are going to dance this evening? It will mean that we will have to stop and speak to other gentlemen and ladies however, rather than keep our own counsel."

Miss Renfrew chuckled. "I suppose that I should, for, truth be told, I am meant to be finding a match for myself this Season and I cannot do that unless I actually integrate myself with others present."

"I suppose that is true," Rachel laughed. "Now, tell me if there are any gentlemen present that you might be considering. There are so many of them! I am sure you could get your dance card entirely filled, should you desire it!"

"I am not certain that I do, for then I shall have no time whatsoever to speak with you!" came the reply. "Though look, there is Lord Wrexham approaching. I think I should be very glad to speak with him."

Rachel glanced to her friend, interest lifting her eyebrow but there was no time for her to say what was in her thoughts for Lord Wrexham had already approached and was now bowing towards them both.

"Good evening, Miss Renfrew, Miss Grifford," he said, his smile broad. "What a pleasant evening this is! What a jovial evening!"

"Indeed it is," Miss Renfrew replied, throwing a quick look towards Rachel who only smiled. "I have heard that Lord Richardson's balls are meant to be the most wonderful of all."

"I think they are, yes," Lord Wrexham replied, "though I think my evening would be all the more delightful if you would agree to dance with me, Miss Renfrew." He smiled and then quickly turned his attention to Rachel, his eyes flaring for a moment as though he feared she thought she had been forgotten. "And you also, of course, Miss Grifford."

"How very generous of you, Lord Wrexham." Rachel waited until Miss Renfrew had slipped her dance card from her wrist and thereafter, did the same. She was quite certain that Lord Wrexham was interested in furthering his connection with Miss Renfrew, for she had seen the flicker of interest in his eyes when he had come to greet them both. And it was no coincidence that he had asked Miss Renfrew for her dance card first! Whether Miss Renfrew noticed that or not, Rachel was not certain, but she was sure that interest would grow all the more, should Miss Renfrew encourage it.

"The quadrille for you, Miss Grifford," Lord Wrexham murmured, handing Rachel back her dance card, "and the waltz for you, Miss Renfrew. I... I presume that is quite all right? I was not certain if you have permission to dance the waltz as yet?"

Miss Renfrew laughed though Rachel noticed the flush of color which instantly came into her cheeks. "I have permission," she said, softly. "I thank you for your consideration, Lord Wrexham. That is very kind of you. I do not think I have danced the waltz as yet this Season."

"Then I am all the more honoured," Lord Wrexham replied, quietly. "I thank you, Miss Grifford, Miss Renfrew. I look forward to our dances. I – ah, good evening, Your Grace! I was not certain that you would be attending this evening."

Rachel turned her head, a spike of energy rushing up her frame as she took in the Duke's dark expression. He was not smiling. Rather, he was scowling as though what had been offered to him by way of greeting was most displeasing.

"You know very well that I was to be in attendance this evening," he said, still scowling. "I told you so myself earlier today."

"Ah, but that did not offer me any certainty," came the reply as Miss Renfrew and Rachel shared a glance. "Though I am glad to see you here. I was just now speaking with Miss Renfrew and Miss Grifford, as you can see."

"I can see that." The Duke did not so much as smile, coming to stand by Lord Wrexham and letting his dark eyes flicker from Rachel to Miss Grifford and back again. "Good evening."

"Good evening," Miss Renfrew replied quickly, though Rachel only nodded. "Are you intending to dance this evening?"

Rachel snatched in a breath, a little astonished at how audacious Miss Renfrew was. It was not as though she herself wanted to dance with the Duke and she was sure that Miss Renfrew did not have any intention of doing so either.

The Duke snorted. "No, I have no intention of dancing this evening, Miss Renfrew. I find it quite a waste of time."

"A waste of time?" Rachel found herself saying, as the Duke turned his attention to her again, sending another wave of awareness rushing through her. "Then why do you attend a ball at all, if it is not to dance?"

The Duke of Longford opened his mouth and then snapped it shut again, perhaps uncertain as to what answer to give. His eyes narrowed as though she was the problem, as though she was the reason for his inability to answer, though Rachel only held his gaze with as much strength as she could, refusing to look away.

"There... there are card games," he said eventually, clearing his throat as he spoke. "I may join them."

"That is most disappointing," Miss Renfrew replied, a smile on her face and a glint in her eye. "I am sure that many a young lady would be eager to dance with a Duke and yet, here you are, refusing to do so."

With a roll of his eyes, the Duke of Longford let out a long and obvious sigh, as though Miss Renfrew's remarks were not even worth considering.

"I quite agree, Miss Renfrew," Lord Wrexham replied, a broad smile settling across his face as he looked at the lady rather than to the Duke himself. "A Duke ought to spend his time dancing and conversing with the young ladies of the *ton*, for that will bring them a great deal of happiness, will it not?"

"I am afraid that I care very little about bringing happiness to others," the Duke interrupted, before either Rachel or Miss Renfrew could reply. "I am not inclined to dance and thus, I shall not."

"A great pity indeed," Miss Renfrew sighed, though she laughed as she said it in clear response to the Duke's angry scowl. "Though I confess that I am very contented with the dances I have at present and would not be particularly enamoured with dancing with a Duke."

Rachel's heart clattered as the Duke's eyebrow lifted, his scowl quickly fading as his eyes then turned towards her. He waited, that eyebrow lifting all the higher as though he were waiting for her either to agree with her friend or say otherwise. She licked her lips, her mouth a little dry, struggling to know what to say.

"I – I would be accepting of anyone who wished to dance with me," she said, eventually, "though I highly doubt that my dance card will be filled this evening."

"I am sure that is not true," Lord Wrexham said immediately, though Rachel offered him a small smile but shook her head, quite certain that was she had said was the truth of the matter. "You are going to be approached by a good many gentlemen during the course of the evening, I am quite sure of it."

"You are very kind," Rachel replied, relieved that she was no longer required to speak to the Duke of Longford directly. "However, my mother is not inclined towards introducing me to any gentlemen or ladies present and therefore, I cannot have the same expectation."

"That is disappointing, I am sure," Lord Wrexham replied though Rachel herself immediately tried to laugh, throwing that remark aside. Perhaps she ought not to have said anything.

"I think you *must* sign Miss Grifford's dance card now, Your Grace." Lord Wrexham turned his attention towards Rachel, his eyes steady and a little grave. "Come now, there can be nothing wrong with dancing only *one* dance. After all, Miss Renfrew has stated that she does not want to dance and therefore, the only person you would be standing up with would be Miss Grifford!"

"Oh no, I should not like to trouble His Grace," Rachel said quickly, her face bursting into flame as she shook her head quickly, seeing the way the Duke frowned. "That is a kind thought, Lord Wrexham, but I did not say any of that in order to encourage His Grace to dance. I only spoke the truth such as it was."

"I see." Lord Wrexham smiled at her and then turned his attention back towards the Duke of Longford in clear expectation of him saying something. Rachel could not bring herself to look at him, however, her face still burning hot, her eyes dancing from one place to the next rather than look the Duke of Longford in the face. She ought not to have said any such thing as that, ought not to have said a word about dancing or her mother or the like, for no doubt the Duke of Longford would now believe that she had been attempting to manipulate him into signing her dance card – which was precisely the opposite of what she wanted.

"It is as Lord Wrexham has said," the Duke muttered, eventually. "I am sure your dance card will be filled very soon, Miss Grifford."

"Though I am the very first to have signed it," Lord Wrexham murmured out of the corner of his mouth – perhaps spoken so quietly so that Rachel would not hear it but Rachel heard it nonetheless, her whole being seeming to erupt into flames of embarrassment. "I am sure that if the Duke of Longford was seen standing up with the lady, then Miss Grifford would have no difficulty in securing other dances."

"You ask too much, Lord Wrexham," the Duke replied, just loud enough for Rachel to hear. "I have already made myself clear. I have no intention of dancing this evening, not even for some poor little miss who cannot find other gentlemen to dance with her."

Tears began to burn in Rachel's eyes at this and she turned away without so much as a word of excusal. The Duke had truly injured her with his harshness and tears began to drip down onto her cheeks, her chest tight as sobs threatened to break through. She heard Miss Renfrew's voice beside her, felt her arm around her shoulders but she could say nothing for fear that her tears would begin to pour with great rapidity. Her heart aching, she permitted Miss Renfrew to guide her to the back of the ballroom where, once more, she stepped into the shadows and allowed them to cover her. This, Rachel supposed, as a handkerchief was pressed into her hand, was precisely where a young lady such as herself, belonged.

Chapter Six

"What is the matter with you?"

Andrew frowned, seeing the anger burning in his friend's eyes. "Whatever is the matter?"

"Are you being genuine in your question?" Lord Wrexham demanded, throwing up his hands. "Pray tell, are you genuinely earnest in your statement?"

"Of course I am." Andrew's frown grew bigger, taking in the way his friend almost exploded with exasperation. "I do not understand what the trouble is."

"The trouble is that you have just insulted Miss Grifford!" Turning, Lord Wrexham flung out one arm in the direction the ladies had gone. "Did you not see that?"

Andrew hesitated, a swarm of guilt beginning to wrap around his heart. "I – I could not say."

"That is nonsense and you know it is so," came the immediate reply. "I know full well that you recognise that what you did and what you said only a few minutes ago was injurious to Miss Grifford. Or did you not notice the way her eyes flooded with tears?"

Something struck hard at Andrew's heart. "She was crying?"

"She was very close to it, thanks to you." Lord Wrexham let out a hiss of breath, shaking his head, his hands at his waist. "Do you not understand? Your words struck her hard and I cannot understand why you thought to say them."

Andrew swallowed back his sharp reply, wanting to immediately absolve himself of any sort of responsibility, wanting to tell Lord Wrexham that he had done nothing wrong but finding that he could not. He had permitted his frustration to take a hold of him, had allowed the embarrassment he felt to run words from his lips that he would never otherwise have said though he certainly had never intended for there to be such a grave injury to Miss Grifford.

"I did not think she would overhear," he muttered, looking away rather than back into the face of his angry friend. "I thought the noise of the ballroom would hide my words."

"Well, it did not. You struck a painful blow to the lady and she disappeared from our company in an instant. That is because of you." Lord Wrexham shook his head again, then passed one hand over his eyes. "I do not think I can spend another moment in your company."

"What do you mean?" Andrew took a step back, seeing the anger still rippling through Lord Wrexham's features and not understanding it in any way whatsoever. After all it was not as though he had brought any insult to Lord Wrexham himself! "I have not upset you, have I?"

"Yes, you have."

"In what way?" Andrew exclaimed, his eyes rounding a little. "I have already told you that it was unintentional and I must say, I did not insult *you* in any way, did I? Why, then would you step away from me?"

Lord Wrexham turned to face him, looking him straight in the eye. "Your Grace, we have been friends for some time – and, I consider, good friends – and yet you do not seem to understand what it is that I am saying. I have already spoken to you about the dark reputation that you are garnering for yourself and warned you against it. Now, however, I see that you have given this no thought whatsoever for, in speaking as you have done, in showing so little consideration as you have done, has only *added* to that reputation. You have injured Miss Grifford tremendously and even now, as I stand here and speak to you, it seems that you do not understand it. Can you not see that there are consequences to speaking so thoughtlessly? Even I do not want to be in company with you and that ought to be something that should trouble you!"

"You... you think I did wrong?"

"Yes!" Lord Wrexham exclaimed, throwing up his hands. "Of course I do! You ought to have signed the lady's dance card! You ought to have stepped out with her rather than insult her."

Andrew shook his head. "If *you* had not said a single word about my dancing, if *you* had not made any suggestion that I dance with the lady, then none of this would have happened."

"I thought you would have a little compassion," came the quick reply. "I saw how you spoke to her – and to her mother – when Lady Carmichael seemed to ignore her own daughter in favour of the other one. I thought there was a little hint of compassion there in your heart for her. I thought you would see just how much dancing with the lady would mean to her. Do you not understand what she was saying? Do you not see that her sister is given preference? Do you not see how the elder Miss Grifford is favoured? Did you not even notice how both Miss Renfrew and she stood together without a single chaperone for either of them?"

Andrew frowned, his heart beginning to hit hard in his chest. "I... I did not."

"Goodness." Lord Wrexham closed his eyes. "No doubt you were so focused upon yourself, upon your own considerations and frustrations with me in how I spoke that you did not even think about Miss Renfrew or Miss Grifford. Had you even taken in what it was she was saying? Had you even thought about the sadness that such a situation must bring her? I could hear it in her voice and see it in her expression, though she laughed and did her best to hide it."

Dropping his head forward, Andrew felt nothing but shame and guilt crash into him, leaving him feeling a little breathless.

"I cannot be any longer in your company," Lord Wrexham continued, firmly. "Not this evening. I am much too angry and, quite frankly, when others who will, no doubt, have heard what you said to her begin to whisper it amongst themselves, I should very much like to be no longer in your company for fear that the rumours will pull me in also."

Andrew lifted his head. "I do not think that anyone will have overheard."

"Then you are a fool," Lord Wrexham declared, firmly, his gaze steady and filled with steel shards. "If Miss Grifford overheard it – and she did – then I can promise you that a good many others will have heard it also. This ballroom is full of both gentlemen and ladies – it is bustling! Someone will have heard you and the whispers will soon begin. I only pray that Miss Grifford will not be marred by them."

Before Andrew could say anything more, his friend had turned sharply on his heel and was gone from him.

Andrew did not know what to do. The shock of his friend's actions was quite astonishing, for Andrew had never been left to stand alone in such a way before. His stomach dipped, his heart beating a little faster as he slowly turned around and began to meander towards the back of the room, attempting to look as nonchalant as possible even though he was feeling a little sick to his stomach. He had been genuine when he had stated that there had been no deliberate act on his part to upset Miss Grifford, having had no intention of allowing her to overhear him though, given that she had, Andrew had not had any expectation that she would be so deeply upset by it! Still scowling, he continued on into the dark recesses of the ballroom, only to come face to face with Miss Grifford herself.

She was standing alone, a handkerchief in one hand and the other grasped into a tight fist which, no doubt, came from the sight of seeing him again. Andrew cleared his throat and looked away, not quite certain whether he ought to say something or simply move away.

"Miss Grifford." Seeing that he had, evidently, decided to say something, Andrew then fought to know how to continue. Closing his eyes, he shrugged and then spread out both hands. "I did not mean to injure you."

"You did not mean to?" Her voice was thin, whispering but yet filled with disbelief. Disbelief which Andrew could very well understand.

"Yes." He lifted both shoulders and then let them fall. "It was not my intention to injure you, Miss Grifford."

She shook her head, her hand now gripping the handkerchief very hard indeed. "I hardly think that you cannot understand how saying such things would not bring me a great injury. I am already well aware that I struggle to have gentlemen offering to dance with me, Your Grace. I am not well known amongst society and shall have very little opportunity to be so, I fear. Therefore, your words could not have struck a harder blow."

"That was unintentional."

The way she looked away told him that she did not believe a word of what he had said and that, for whatever reason, irritated Andrew a great deal.

"I am speaking the truth, Miss Grifford. I spoke honestly and –"

"That is your issue there, Your Grace." Miss Grifford lifted her chin, her eyes sharp and no longer filled with tears. "You may very well be honest – I believe that I said I have understood your words to be quite true – but what you seem to be lacking is the understanding that what you said to me was greatly injurious." She took a step closer to him, one hand pointing, her finger pressing lightly against his chest. "Do you not think that I am already aware of such things? That they do not cause me pain? That my heart is not already aching? Whether you were honest or not, do you not see that your words have struck a painful blow to an already broken heart?"

Andrew swallowed tightly, waiting for the rush of frustration and anger which her words would, no doubt, bring about but much to his surprise, they did not come. In fact, nothing but sympathy filled his heart and his hand, seemingly of its own accord, reached up and took hers as her finger pressed heavily against his heart.

"I am sorry."

The touch of his hand on hers seemed to alter her expression almost instantly for her eyes flared with surprise and shock. Andrew pressed her hand, a strange desire within him not to release her hand from his.

"I should have been more considerate," he admitted, after a few minutes. "Forgive me, Miss Grifford."

Her mouth opened and shut without a word escaping from it though her eyes were still round with surprise. When he finally released her hand, Miss Grifford took a step back from him, both hands clutched together at her heart.

"And I shall dance with you, if you will permit it," he said, surprising himself all the more with his astonishing words. "The waltz, perhaps? That way, you can be certain that many gentlemen and ladies of the *ton* will wish to become acquainted with you."

The way his mind screamed at him gave him pause but there was nothing that that he could say now. The words had been spoken, the offer had been made and now it was up to Miss Grifford to answer.

"You would be willing to dance with me only out of pity?"

Andrew hesitated and that, evidently, was enough of an answer for Miss Grifford, given the way she looked away, an exclamation on her lips.

"Not out of pity," he said quickly, though it was already much too late. "No, not at all out of pity."

"Then to assuage your conscience," she responded, hoarsely. "It is not to make me feel better, it is to make yourself feel better."

Andrew threw up his hands. "What do you want from me, Miss Grifford? I have come to apologise, have I not? I have come to seek you out, to make right – or to attempt to make right – what I know to be wrong. Is that not enough for you?"

Miss Grifford drew herself up, her arms folding over her chest as she looked him dead in the eye. "I would not have you pity me, Your Grace," she said, though her voice still held the edge of pain. "I would not have your pity nor would I have you using me to make your own guilt a little lesser. I would be valued for the lady that I am rather than being treated with such disdain." She closed her eyes tightly. "Though it appears to me that you will treat me just as my own mother and father do, Your Grace, and make me very little in your eyes, given your dark reputation, perhaps that is just what I ought to expect."

She said nothing more but turned away from him at once, leaving his mouth to fall open in shock as he fought to find an answer – but it was much too late. His own heart clamoured within him, pain dragging through him as he fought back against the shame which threatened to overwhelm him. He had caused her a great injury by speaking without much consideration but her words now threw heavy darts back into his own heart – darts which he could not seem to remove from himself. Her words held so much truth, he could barely breathe for a moment. It seemed he *was* gaining a dark reputation amongst the *ton* and after what he had not only said but done to Miss Grifford, Andrew could finally understand why.

Chapter Seven

"How are you this afternoon, my dear friend?"

Rachel smiled quickly, wanting to reassure Miss Renfrew. "I am quite well, I thank you."

"Are you sure?"

She nodded. "I enjoyed last evening," she lied, trying to put a light tone into her voice that she did not truly feel. "The ball was not a complete disaster and I did end up dancing four dances."

Miss Renfrew smiled though her eyes still held a great deal of worry. "That was good, certainly. Lord Wrexham was very kind to us both."

Rachel caught the slight softness about her friend's eyes and found her interest piqued. "You do think well of Lord Wrexham, do you not?"

Miss Renfrew's gaze quickly turned away from her. "I think him a very kind gentleman, yes."

"But more than that?" Rachel wondered aloud, seeing how her friend flushed. "Is there a spark of interest there?"

With a small sigh, Miss Renfrew looked away. "I could not say for certain," she said, her voice a little light which made Rachel quite certain that there was more to what she said than she was willing to admit to. "There is a kindness to him which I deeply value. It is not often found in gentlemen, I think."

"That is probably very true," Rachel admitted, her thoughts immediately going to the Duke of Longford, "though I do not know the gentlemen of society very well as yet, I confess." She smiled as Miss Renfrew finally caught her gaze again. "I think Lord Wrexham does have an interest in you also, I must say."

"Do you?" Hope filled Miss Renfrew's eyes as Rachel nodded fervently. "Are you quite certain? What would give you that sort of idea?"

Rachel laughed softly, her heart lifting a little as she saw the excitement in her friend's face. "It was only a very brief consideration," she said, grinning, "but I did see his gaze linger upon you on more than one occasion. That must speak of interest, surely?"

"Mayhap." Miss Renfrew shrugged though there was a glimmer of a smile there. "Thank you for telling me. I do think that Lord Wrexham is a very kind gentleman and I would be glad to be a little more in his company, I must admit." Her eyes settled on Rachel's. "And how are your spirits this afternoon?"

Rachel hesitated, then shook her head. "I am doing my best not to think of what happened," she said, truthfully. "I am trying to lift my spirits for I cannot permit myself to linger on what the Duke of Longford said to me. It would only make my heart all the more painful, I think."

"It was utterly disgraceful." Miss Renfrew's expression grew dark. "I was shocked, I must admit. Horrified that such a gentleman would think to speak to you in such a way."

Rachel managed a wry smile though her heart was suddenly all the more pained at the recollection. "He did come to speak with me, in what I think was an attempt to apologise," she said, making her friend's eyes round. "Do you know that he asked me to dance with him at the very end of our conversation?" Seeing Miss Renfrew's eyes flare, Rachel nodded and then shook her head. "It was quite ridiculous. He asked me only to assuage his conscience, I am sure, for his apology was not even truly an apology!"

"And you refused him?"

"Yes, I did." Rachel let out a slow breath and then closed her eyes. "Perhaps I ought not to have done but I could not bear the thought of being in his arms. That gentleman has such a dark demeanour about him that I could not imagine being swept into a waltz with him!"

"He asked to dance the waltz?"

Rachel let out a broken laugh and rolled her eyes. "Could you imagine it? The young lady who is almost always tossed aside, ignored and forgotten by even her own family, standing up with a Duke? Even the thought is preposterous."

"I should not say so," Miss Renfrew replied, smiling an encouragement towards Rachel. "I think you would do very well dancing with a Duke… although mayhap not the Duke of Longford!"

Both Rachel and she laughed at this, making Rachel's spirits lift again. Turning their conversation towards other matters, Miss Renfrew and she continued on in their walk for some minutes before, much to Rachel's surprise and, unfortunately, her dislike, they came upon three gentlemen standing together – and the Duke of Longford was one of the three. She shot a look towards Miss Renfrew but given that one of the remaining gentlemen was Lord Wrexham, Rachel realized there was very little chance that she would be able to drag her friend away from the group.

They would be forced to stand and speak with them all, though mayhap she might be able to ignore the Duke of Longford without making that in itself too obvious.

"Good afternoon, Miss Renfrew, Miss Grifford!" Lord Wrexham was immediately welcoming, his gaze fixing itself to Miss Renfrew almost at once. "How pleasant to find you both out here together."

"I thank you," Rachel managed to murmur, though her eyes went to the other gentleman beside Lord Wrexham. She did not know him though he had a pleasant face with a warm smile and deep green eyes. She offered him a demure smile and then looked to the Duke, though that look did not linger long.

"Should we make some introductions?" Lord Wrexham asked, still smiling and gesturing to the gentleman that Rachel did not recognize. "Your Grace?"

The Duke of Longford cleared his throat and nodded curtly. "Yes, of course. Might I present my cousin, who has come unexpectedly to London? This is the Marquess of Chiddick. Lord Chiddick, might I present Miss Renfrew and Miss Grifford."

Rachel dropped into a curtsy just as the Earl smiled and then bowed his head.

"Good afternoon to you both, I am delighted to make your acquaintance," he said, his voice rich with warmth. "As my cousin has said, I have come to London a little unexpectedly. I was in Bath, you see, but upon hearing the news that my cousin is now in London having been absent from society for some years, I thought it my duty to come and visit. It has been some time since I have seen my cousin and therefore, I thought it a capital idea to both greet him and enjoy the warm society which London can offer me."

Still smiling, Rachel shared a glance with Miss Renfrew who, smiling back at her, then turned again to Lord Chiddick. "I am sure that all of society will be glad to greet you," she said, quickly. "I do hope your cousin will be doing all he can to introduce you to as many gentlemen and ladies as he can so you will begin to receive as many invitations as he does!"

Lord Chiddick laughed along with her and though Rachel threw a quick glance to the Duke of Longford, he was scowling darkly. She shrugged inwardly, thinking silently to herself that if the Duke of Longford wished to be displeased with her, then she cared very little for that. They were not about to be friends now, were they?

"I must hope I am a little more popular than the Duke of Longford," Lord Chiddick said, though his voice was low as though he only wished for her to hear him. "I have heard that his reputation is very difficult indeed."

"I have done nothing to earn such a reputation," came the instant reply and Rachel, without warning, found herself scoffing aloud. Immediately, all three gentlemen's eyes went to hers. Rachel's face exploded with flame and she looked away, her hands clasping lightly in front of her.

"I think that is fair," Lord Wrexham said eventually, shooting her a small smile. "Now, shall we walk together for a short while? I should be very glad to have your company, Miss Renfrew."

"Of course!" Miss Renfrew immediately stepped closer to Lord Wrexham and when he offered his arm, she took it without hesitation, and began to walk along the path with him. Rachel licked her lips, a nervousness beginning to overtake her as she saw the Duke and Lord Chiddick glance at one another. Not wanting them to feel obliged – and certainly because she did not want to walk with the Duke, Rachel forced a smile.

"I think I shall follow after my friend."

"Please."

The two gentlemen both said the same thing at the same time, though Lord Chiddick was the only one who offered his arm to her.

"Please," he said again, as though to overrule the Duke of Longford. "If you would walk with me, I should be very grateful."

"You are most kind." Rachel accepted at once, relieved that her friend had not gone too far ahead. "Thank you, Lord Chiddick."

As she took his arm, Rachel could not help but cast a glance towards the Duke of Longford. His eyebrows were low over his eyes, his brow furrowing and his mouth in a flat line. Could it be that he had wanted to walk with her? No, she told herself, there could be no assumption of that, not after what he had said to her the previous evening. No doubt, he had thought only to walk with her in a further attempt to assuage his own guilt. Rachel was not about to permit him to do that.

"You say you are in London for some time?" Rachel asked, as she settled her hand on Lord Chiddick's. "Might I ask if you intend to linger long here?"

"I do not know." Lord Chiddick sighed but smiled as he did so. "It will depend on the company I keep and how enjoyable a time I am having. Though if *this* new acquaintance is anything to go by, I do not think that I will be leaving London any time soon!"

Rachel felt herself smile at this, her face a little flushed. "I thank you for your kind words, Lord Chiddick. I do hope that you have a very enjoyable time this Season."

"I do expect to dance a great deal," he told her, as Rachel glanced over her shoulder, all too aware of the Duke of Longford's presence walking closely behind them. "Do you dance, Miss Grifford?"

She looked back at him. "I do."

"Capital!" he exclaimed, thrilling her with his exuberance and clear anticipation. "Might I be all the more fortunate and know which ball you are attending this evening… if you are attending a ball, that is!"

Rachel laughed, finding the gentleman very jovial indeed. "I am attending a ball, yes," she said, smiling at the way his eyes filled with a sudden hope. "I am to attend Lord and Lady Hallwright's ball."

Lord Chiddick let out a whoop of delight which made Rachel giggle, for she had never once been in the company of a gentleman such as this, one who was so delighted with almost everything she had to say – and who appeared to be so eager to spend further time in her company.

"Then I shall find you this evening without a moment's hesitation," he promised, reaching across to pat her hand with his as it rested on his arm. "You will save me a dance, I hope?"

"My dance card is never fully filled," she told him, though a little embarrassed to admit it to him. "So yes, I should be glad to dance with you, Lord Chiddick. I will let no-one else sign my dance card until you are found."

Lord Chiddick beamed at her. "I thank you, Miss Grifford. That is truly delightful."

A slight cough came from behind them and Rachel turned her head to see the Duke of Longford lift an eyebrow in her direction. "Might I be permitted to dance with you also?" he asked, his tone a little gruff as his gaze slid away from her.

Rachel's mouth went dry and her steps slowed as she quickly considered. The truth was, she did not want to dance with the Duke of Longford but it would be difficult to refuse him with Lord Chiddick standing so close to them both. If she said she would not, then, no doubt, Lord Chiddick would wonder as to why she had done so and might then ask the Duke of Longford himself about it – and then what would he say? What would *she* say, if he was bold enough to ask her? Rachel swallowed tightly, wondering if the Duke of Longford had asked her such a thing simply because he did not want to give her opportunity to refuse and, in considering it, found herself becoming a little angry.

"I suppose that will be all right," she said, her lip curling just a little, her free hand tightening into a fist as the Duke nodded, giving her not even the smallest smile nor look of appreciation for her consent.

"Wonderful," Lord Chiddick said, clearly not seeing anything that Rachel truly felt. "You shall have your dance card filled this evening, Miss Grifford, I am sure of it!"

Rachel offered him a smile but nothing more, her heart and her spirits sinking low. Lord Chiddick's offer had made her wonderfully delighted but the Duke of Longford's request had quite dulled that all away. This evening was not to be the most wonderful evening of her life thus far, she was quite sure, not when she would have no choice but to step into the arms of the Duke.

Chapter Eight

Why ever did I say that I would dance with her this evening?

Andrew shook his head to himself and then rolled his eyes for good measure. He had spent the last few hours wondering what it was he had done in telling Miss Grifford that he would like to dance with her this evening and thereafter, worrying about whether or not he ought to do as he had stated. The truth was, he had spoken without thinking and, in doing so, had found himself a little astonished at the words which had come out of his mouth. Miss Grifford had also seemed very surprised by his request but had been gracious enough to accept him – though he had seen the confusion in her eyes and had watched her as she hesitated before answering. Either she had been a little confused as to why he had asked her such a thing or she had been trying to find a way to refuse him – and Andrew was quite certain it had been the latter.

"Good evening, Your Grace!"

Andrew turned to see a young lady smiling up at him, a lady beside him who was clearly her mother given the similarity in features. The way that she spoke to him was a clear message of familiarity though Andrew himself could not seem to think of her name or how they had come to be introduced.

He cleared his throat. "Good evening."

"Are you enjoying the ball this evening?" the young lady asked as her mother beamed a smile at him, clearly delighted that they found him entirely unattached to anyone else. "I do hope that you will be dancing, Your Grace, for this is one of the most remarkable balls of the Season thus far, I am sure!"

"Is that so?" Andrew asked, dryly, eyeing the lady and thinking that the only reason she had said such a thing was so that she might find herself in his company and with the hope of dancing with him. "What makes it remarkable, might I ask?"

The young lady's smile fixed to her face as she looked up at him, her eyes rounding just a little as, to his mind, she began to find a reason as to why this evening was more incredible than the other balls of the Season. Her mother nudged her lightly – an action which Andrew did not miss – and Andrew's lip curled just a little.

"As we all know, the Marquess of Hallwright hosts the most remarkable balls," the young lady said eventually, stammering just a little. "I – I believe it has the best entertainments, the very best decorations and the like." Recovering herself a little, she smiled a little more brightly. "And that is why I hope you will dance this evening for I am sure that the *ton* will be speaking of this evening for a long time to come."

Andrew cleared his throat again, this time a little more gruffly and watched as the bright smile began to fade again. He did not know what she expected him to say. Did she think that he would immediately agree, that he would ask for her dance card and thereafter, sign it with a feverish excitement?

"Ah, Your Grace."

A familiar voice caught his attention and he turned his head just to see Miss Grifford standing beside him. She offered him a small smile but then looked to the young lady who had been speaking with him in the first place.

"Forgive me for interrupting your conversation with my sister," she said, saving him from having to ask who this young lady was. A gentle relief flooded him and he nodded curtly, though the reminder that he was to dance with her flooded his mind at the very same time.

"Not at all. Might I have your dance card, Miss Grifford?"

Her eyes rounded in surprise, perhaps having no expectation that he would have remembered that he was to dance with her.

"I presume Lord Chiddick has already found you?" he asked, as she slipped the dance card from her wrist and with a hand that trembled lightly handed it to him. "I should not like to take his place."

She nodded. "Yes, he has," she said faintly, as Andrew saw the other Miss Grifford's eyebrows begin to knot. "As has Lord Wrexham."

"And you did not think that I would remember?" he found himself asking, seeing her eyes drop to the ground and immediately regretting speaking so. She did not need his condemnation. "Mayhap you did not wish me to do so."

"Not in the least," Miss Grifford replied, quickly. "I thank you for your consideration, Your Grace."

"Yes, of *course* she does," the other Miss Grifford said, emphasizing it so strongly, Andrew understood precisely what it was that she was hoping for. It was clear that the other Miss Grifford was hoping for a chance to dance with him also, though Andrew had no intention of giving it. The only reason he was dancing with Miss Grifford was because he had stated he wished to and he was not about to go back on that now and embarrass her even more.

"I confess, I am surprised that you would wish to dance with Rachel rather than asking for Bettina's dance card, Your Grace."

Andrew looked up from where his pencil had been hovering over the dance card, mentally deciding which dance he would take. "I beg your pardon?"

Miss Grifford's mother – Lady Carmichael, if he remembered correctly – was looking back at him with one arched eyebrow.

"I asked why you appear so eager to dance with Rachel when my eldest daughter, Bettina, is standing here," she said again, gesturing to the elder Miss Grifford who immediately smiled and then batted her eyelashes. "Rachel is nothing particularly special, Your Grace, but my eldest Bettina... as you can see..."

Andrew did not know what to say to this. He could not think of what to say, could not imagine what it was that Miss Rachel Grifford was thinking and feeling at this very moment and, as he looked to Miss Bettina Grifford, found his stomach clenching and his heart beginning to pound furiously. Miss Bettina Grifford, rather than showing any sort of embarrassment, being at all disappointed with her mother's words or worried about her sister was, instead, beaming up at him as though what her mother had said was the most incredible thing in all the world. Andrew swallowed the knot in his throat, looking back at Miss Rachel Grifford and seeing how her head dropped low and how her gaze settled to the floor.

Shame swallowed him up and he closed his eyes for a moment, recalling all that he had said to Miss Grifford at the previous ball and realizing now just how fully his words had cut into her.

He was utterly ashamed of himself.

"The polonaise, Miss Grifford?" he said, a little more loudly than he had intended, ignoring both Lady Carmichael and the grinning Miss Bettina Grifford. Putting his pencil to the dance card, he signed his initials for the polonaise and then hesitated. "And the waltz."

He heard the swift intake of breath from Miss Rachel Grifford and caught the way Miss Bettina Grifford looked straight to her mother, her eyes rounding. Finding himself smiling, he handed the dance card back to Miss Rachel Grifford and turned to her fully, ignoring Miss Bettina Grifford entirely.

"I do hope that you will be contented with that?" he asked her, seeing her look up at him with wide eyes. "I will come in search of you later this evening." So saying, he snapped his heels together and then turned to move away.

"Your... your Grace?"

Andrew glanced back over his shoulder, seeing Lady Carmichael's wide eyes staring at him with what appeared to be utter shock in her expression. "Yes, Lady Carmichael?"

"Are... are you...?" She closed her eyes for a moment, drew in a breath and then set her shoulders, gazing up at him. "Might you be dancing with anyone else, Your Grace?"

He shook his head. "No, I do not think so."

"You have no desire to dance with my other daughter?" There was a slight hint of surprise melded with irritation which wrapped through her words, making Andrew's stomach twist.

"I have no intention of dancing with anyone else," he stated, firmly, "save for Miss Renfrew."

"Then... then you will only dance with two young ladies this evening?"

He nodded. "Yes."

"But... " Lady Carmichael seemed to run out of things to say, finding herself staring back at him with such wide eyes, Andrew could not help but smile. She could not question him as to why he was only dancing with two young ladies and certainly could not state that he was doing something wrong by pursuing only these two. Nor could she ask why he was choosing not to dance with her eldest daughter for no one had any right to question a Duke! With a nod, his smile growing a little more, Andrew turned and made his way back through the ballroom, finding a sense of satisfaction growing steadily within him.

Though, he considered, his brow furrowing, he would *have* to find Miss Renfrew and beg a dance from her. If she refused him, he would have to explain that it was only so that the *ton* did not take notice of his two dances with Miss Grifford and surely she would understand that? Thereafter, Andrew considered, he would have to give a genuine apology to Miss Grifford for what he had said to her at the previous ball. It was only now, when he had heard and seen Lady Carmichael's disregard of her, that he had finally realized just how much his words had pained her. Now that he had seen it, now that he understood it, the realization of what he had done swallowed him up with guilt and a true apology was certainly required of him.

And I will give it, he told himself, firmly. *The very moment I take her out to dance, I shall make certain she knows just how sorry I truly am.*

"The polonaise went very well, Miss Grifford, so I can safely assume that our waltz will be the same."

Miss Grifford looked up at him with wide eyes, her lip catching between her teeth and, much to Andrew's surprise, he felt his heart swell suddenly. Whatever this feeling was, whatever sensation had caught him, he was not particularly pleased by it and quickly looked away from her.

"There is something I wish to say to you before we dance," he continued, a little frustrated that he had not managed to find the words before they had danced the polonaise. To his frustration, he had been rather nervous and now that this second opportunity was upon him, Andrew knew he had to take his chance to speak to her all that was on his mind.

"Oh?" Miss Grifford looked up at him but then pulled her gaze away from him again just as quickly.

"Yes, I... " *Why do I find this so difficult to say?* He harrumphed and then turned, stepping back from her so they might bow and curtsy to one another before the waltz began. "I must apologise for what I said to you at the previous ball."

"You have apologised already, Your Grace."

"Yes, but not with any sincerity," he admitted, a little darkly. "I see now that my words must have cut right through you, must have caused you a great deal of pain and for that, I am truly sorry. I ought never to have said a word and indeed, I believe that I did so out of frustration and irritation. I did not want to dance and I was frustrated with Lord Wrexham's attempts to encourage me to do so but all the same, I should never have said a single word to you in that regard." He put one hand to his heart and then bowed low. "I beg your forgiveness, Miss Grifford."

She blinked at him and then sank into her curtsy, as was required and expected before their waltz. "I thank you for your honesty, Your Grace. It is much appreciated."

"I mean every word," he swore, seeing a small smile tilt up one side of her mouth. "I am being entirely genuine, Miss Grifford."

"And I believe you," she said, simply. "If you recall, Your Grace, I was very well able to distinguish that your attitude previously was not as it ought to have been."

He found himself smiling, a little relieved that she was so amenable to his apology. "Yes, I do recall that," he agreed, quietly. "You were able to speak very frankly to me – not that I did not deserve that, however."

She laughed then and Andrew took the opportunity to step forward and take her up in his arms as the music for the waltz began. The laughter lingered in her expression as they stepped about the floor together, softening into a gentle smile as the steps they took together seemed to merge into one. There was no tugging this way and that, no mistaking one step for another. Instead, there was a beautiful simplicity in their dance, as though they both knew exactly what the other was thinking and were able to anticipate the next step each person took. His arm tightened around her just a little, the other hand holding tight to hers as he looked down into her eyes.

His heart slammed hard against his ribs and Andrew sucked in air, his breathing rapidly quickening. Whatever was happening here? What was this strange warmth which now flooded his heart? It could not only be sympathy, could it? He had felt sympathy and sorrow before, had he not? This was certainly not at all what he had felt like at that time, so what was this new, strange sensation?

Fear reached up over his shoulder and wrapped cold fingers around his heart. The dance came to an end and when Miss Grifford sighed contentedly and stepped back from him, Andrew found himself frowning. He bowed, and he offered her his arm as he ought and then led her back to her mother, but he did not dare say a word – not when his mind was whirring through the various sensations which now poured through him.

This had been a dreadful idea, he told himself, forcing a smile as he bowed and then hurriedly stepped away. Dancing with Miss Grifford was something he could never dare do again for fear that whatever was going on in his heart at present would only increase until it became something that would never leave his heart again.

Chapter Nine

"We have to speak, Rachel."

Rachel looked up from her embroidery. "Yes, Mama?"

"The Duke of Longford."

Her mother came a little further into the room and then sat down, her hands clasped in her lap though her eyes were fixed to Rachel's with a fervency which Rachel did not like in the least. There was no smile upon her mother's face and indeed, the way she looked at her made Rachel feel as though she had done something wrong.

She chose to say nothing, waiting until her mother chose to speak again and praying that this conversation would not lead her into any sort of difficulty.

"The Duke of Longford danced twice with you last evening," her mother said eventually, her tone grating. "Why?"

Rachel blinked in surprise. "I do not understand what you mean, Mama."

"Why did he choose to dance with you?"

"I do not know."

Lady Carmichael narrowed her gaze just a little. "He said something about Lord Chadwick – "

"Lord Chiddick," Rachel corrected quickly, seeing her mother's face beginning to turn red. "He is the Duke's cousin. Miss Renfrew and I were introduced to him when we took our walk in the park."

Lady Carmichael drew herself up. "And you did not think to introduce this Marquess to your sister?"

Rachel blinked and then frowned. "I had no opportunity, Mama. You took Bettina to go in search of someone – I do not know who – and Miss Renfrew and I walked together around the ballroom. Lord Chiddick then found us, signed our dance cards – as did Lord Wrexham – and when Miss Renfrew had to take her leave for the dance, I then spied both Bettina and you and returned to join you both."

This did not appear to be a good enough explanation for Lady Carmichael, however, for she narrowed her eyes, tossed her head and then rose to her feet. "It is quite incomprehensible to me that the Duke of Longford would stand up with you but refuse to even consider Bettina."

The harsh words crashed into Rachel's heart and she looked away, aware of the feeling of tears clogging her throat.

"You have shown your sister very little consideration by not insisting at once that she come to be introduced to the Marquess of Chiddick," Lady Carmichael continued. "Do you not understand how important it is for your sister to be well known amongst the *ton*? Everyone must see her beauty and her finesse! That way, the gentlemen of London will be eager to pursue her and she will have her choice of suitors."

Rachel swallowed her tears, took in a breath and looked up at her mother. "And what about me?"

It was the first time she had ever dared say something to that effect and the way her mother's eyes narrowed told Rachel that she had set foot into dangerous territory. Evidently, her mother believed that what she was doing by showing favoritism towards Bettina was quite fair and Rachel, in questioning that, was doing a great wrong.

"What about you, Rachel?" Lady Carmichael put her hands to her hips. Her eyes spitting shards of glass. "You have attended every ball we have done together, have we not? You have been introduced to various gentlemen, you have danced with – "

"No, Mama." Aware of the shaking within her soul, Rachel forced the words out, telling herself to be brave. "I have not been introduced to various gentlemen. That has been Bettina. You have chosen *her* to go and greet various gentlemen whereas I have been left to stand in the shadows. Do you not recall, at our debut ball, how you were eager for me to wait for your return and then, during the course of the entire ball, you did not come back in search of me once?" She watched as her mother's hands fell to her sides, though her eyes remained fixed and angry. Emboldened, Rachel continued on regardless, forcing the words from her mouth. "I have not been given the same opportunities as Bettina, Mama. Yes, I have danced a good many dances but that has only been because the gentlemen I have danced with are of my own acquaintance. Miss Renfrew has been my support in that before you think that there has been anything improper, but I can assure you that it is not because of *your* doing that I have found myself dancing. I understand that Bettina takes a great deal of your attention and your time but that does not mean that I ought to be forgotten."

Lady Carmichael paused, her eyes rounding as though she had never once realized what it was she was doing as regarded Rachel. "I – I do not think that I forget you," she began, though there was no anger in her tone now but rather a confusion, a hesitation there instead. "Bettina *ought* to come first because she is the eldest, however." She nodded, though half to herself as though to confirm that what she was thinking was quite correct. "Which means that you still ought to make sure that she is introduced to the very same gentlemen that you are acquainted with. *And* you must make certain that the Duke of Longford dances with her!"

"And how can I do that?" Rachel got to her feet, exasperated and upset that despite her boldness, her mother did not seem to understand in the least what it was that she was saying. "What is it that you expect me to say to the Duke of Longford to force him to dance with Bettina? Do not think for a moment that I have any sort of hold or influence upon the Duke, Mama! I was as astonished as both Bettina and yourself at how he asked me to dance. I did not think for a moment that he would truly do so – and certainly not the waltz either!"

Lady Carmichael held Rachel's gaze for some moments, as though she were sure that Rachel was not telling the truth for some reason. Rachel returned it steadily, however, whispering courageous words to herself inwardly until, finally, Lady Carmichael sighed and shook her head.

"Bettina is most upset that the Duke of Longford refused to stand up with her." Lady Carmichael walked across the room and sat down heavily in a chair, her shoulders rounding and her hands clasped in her lap as her head dropped forward. "I do not understand it."

Rachel did not know what to make of this. Either her mother was stating that she did not understand why the Duke of Longford would stand up with Rachel rather than Bettina or she did not understand why Bettina would be so very upset about it all. Rachel was quite certain, however, that it was the former rather than the latter. Though her mother was upset, Rachel did not believe that she had truly taken in anything that Rachel herself had said and that made her heart sink all the lower.

"There you are." The door swung open and Bettina marched in, her arms folding across her chest as she narrowed her eyes, fixing them to Rachel. "*You* need to explain yourself."

"I have nothing to explain." Rachel sat back down and then picked up her embroidery. "Should I ring for tea, Mama?"

"Yes, I think that would be wise." Lady Carmichael rose to her feet and went to ring the bell rather than permitting Rachel to do it. "There may be gentlemen callers this afternoon, Bettina, so please do sit down and make sure you are prepared for them. I – "

"What has Rachel said by way of explanation?" Bettina demanded, interrupting her mother and glaring still at Rachel. "Why did she set the Duke of Longford away from me?"

Rachel lifted an eyebrow at her sister and then returned her gaze to her mother who shook her head.

"Your sister did not say a single word to the Duke of Longford about you, I am sure," Lady Carmichael said, sounding weary and fatigued. "The Duke of Longford, as you know, is a gentleman who has a darkness about him. Everyone in society is speaking of it. He is the gentleman who stands at the back of the ballroom, who glares at those who come to speak with him and who has not even the smallest kindness on his lips for any living soul. Why, then, should you be so upset by his lack of consideration? It does not matter."

"Yes, it does!" Bettina exclaimed, throwing out one hand towards Rachel. "He ought not to be greeting, dancing and smiling at my sister when *I* am present! What is it that he does not see in me that he sees in her? It is utterly preposterous to think that he has any sort of enjoyment in her company over mine and yet he appeared so disinclined towards me that I am quite sure that Rachel said something to him! Something that was most untrue, I am sure. I –"

A knock came to the door and Lady Carmichael quickly called for them to enter, no doubt thinking that it was the maid with the tea tray. Instead, much to Rachel's surprise, the butler hurried in and handed Lady Carmichael two calling cards.

Lady Carmichael let out a muffled exclamation and put one hand over her mouth, her eyes wide as she stared first at Rachel and then looked to Bettina.

"What is it, Mama?" Rachel asked, the tears which had begun to burn in her eyes over her sister's cruel remarks beginning to fade away. "What is it?"

"It is... " Lady Carmichael drew in a breath, rose to her feet and nodded to the butler. "But of course. At once." Lowering her voice, she hissed to Bettina to go to stand by a chair and then urged them both to pinch their cheeks. Rachel did so rather reluctantly, though her thoughts continually turned to who it might be that had come to call.

She did not have to wonder for long.

"The Marquess of Chiddick and His Grace, the Duke of Longford," the butler announced, as Bettina let out a squeak of excitement, clearly believing that they had come to see them both. Rachel's stomach began to twist itself in knots, her heart pounding as she saw the Duke's gaze immediately turned to her. He bowed but kept his gaze fixed to hers, as though she was the only one he had wanted to see.

"Your Grace," Lady Carmichael exclaimed, though her voice was a little breathless. "Please do come in. Is this your cousin? I must confess that we are not yet acquainted and I am so dreadfully sorry that has not happened as yet."

"Not at all," the Duke replied, though again, he did not take his gaze from Rachel and she, in return, could do nothing but look back at him. "Lady Carmichael, Miss Bettina Grifford, might I present my cousin, the Marquess of Chiddick."

Bettina dropped into the most wonderful curtsy while Rachel only bobbed a quick curtsy in return, having already been acquainted with the Marquess. Her mouth went dry as the Duke managed a small smile, wondering why it was that he had thought to come to call. Did he not know what difficulties his visit would bring? Or mayhap his cousin had been the one eager to call upon them and thus, out of loyalty to his family, he had chosen to do so, albeit unwillingly?

"Please, do sit down," she found herself saying when both her mother and her sister remained silent – perhaps in awe of their company. "We have just rung for a tea tray so it should be with us very soon."

"Capital!" Lord Chiddick said, making Rachel smile as both the Duke and he took a seat, though the Duke sat closer to Rachel than Lord Chiddick, who chose to take a seat opposite her and therefore, closer to Bettina. "I am delighted that we were able to call upon you all. I did enjoy the ball a great deal last evening, Miss Grifford, and was very pleased indeed to be able to stand up with you."

"Thank you, Lord Chiddick," Rachel replied, managing a small smile even though uncertainty and confusion wound its way around her heart for not only was Lord Chiddick directing his attention towards her, the Duke of Longford had barely taken his gaze from her – a fact that, no doubt, her sister would be very well aware of. "It was a most enjoyable evening."

"Did *you* enjoy last evening, Your Grace?" Bettina asked, her voice dripping with sweetness, her eyes smiling at him though the Duke of Longford gave her only the smallest of glances. "I do hope it was a pleasant evening for you."

The Duke hesitated and then shrugged. "It was not a bad evening, certainly. I am not usually a gentleman who steps out to dance but the three dances I partook in were not as dreadful as I had imagined they would be."

"Three?" Bettina asked, her eyes turning towards Rachel again though Rachel did not understand why. "So you danced two dances with my sister and only one with Miss Renfrew?"

Rachel flushed, immediately understanding why her sister was so concerned. To have such attention from the Duke was worthy of note in any other circumstances, though Rachel alone understood why the Duke had decided to dance twice with her. Bettina did not realize it, of course, but it was because of how their mother and she had decided to speak to Rachel that the Duke had shown such generosity.

"I believe that I can dance with whomever I decide, Miss Grifford." The Duke's voice had dropped in tone, his eyebrows knotting as he looked back steadily at Bettina. "Is there something about that which troubles you?"

Bettina opened her mouth and then closed it again, sending a look towards Rachel who merely lifted her shoulders gently and then let them fall, fully aware that there was a sudden tension in the room. This was broken by the arrival of the maid and the tea tray, leaving Lady Carmichael to swoop in and thereafter, encourage Bettina to serve the tea to them all. It was her responsibility as the eldest and Rachel found herself rather relieved that she was able to sit back and watch the proceedings rather than having to take part. Bettina was doing her best to smile and appear jovial but Rachel could tell that there was a great deal of concern there. The way her sister's eyes darted to the Duke and then away from him spoke of her nervousness. Was she still trying to capture the Duke's attention? Or was she simply worried about how the Duke would now respond to her, given his last few sharp words to her?

"You said you are the Duke of Longford's cousin?" Lady Carmichael asked, speaking to Lord Chiddick who nodded profusely. "How wonderful to have you here in London with us! I am sure that society will be very glad to have your company."

"It has been very pleasant thus far," Lord Chiddick agreed. "I actually spent the first month in Bath before coming to London. When I heard that my cousin was here, I wanted very much to be in his company again."

"How very generous!" Lady Carmichael exclaimed. "To wish to be with family is a strong blessing indeed."

"Yes it is." Lord Chiddick passed a look to the Duke but the gentleman's expression barely changed. In fact, there was only a momentary flicker in his eyes rather than any sort of appreciation or joy. The dark demeanor had returned. Why, Rachel wondered, had these two gentlemen come to call? It was not as though the Duke appeared to be at all glad to be in their company, which made her wonder if Lord Chiddick had practically forced his cousin to come with him. Her heart twisted a little at the thought, as though she had somehow eagerly desired the Duke of Longford to *want* to call upon her, though that idea was entirely preposterous.

"We are very good friends as well as relatives," Lord Chiddick stated, picking up his tea cup and taking a small sip from it before he put it back down on the table again. "Is that not so, Your Grace?"

The Duke of Longford grunted. "I suppose so."

"When were you last in company with each other?" Lady Carmichael asked, as Rachel sipped her tea. "Has it been recent?"

The two gentlemen looked at each other and Rachel was sure she caught the Duke of Longford give a small shake of his head.

Lord Chiddick, however, did not appear to see it.

"It was at a sad event," he said, slowly, "at the passing of the Duke's late father under most troubling circumstances."

The Duke of Longford immediately cleared his throat and then let his gaze bounce around the room. "That was a difficult time."

"And under troubling circumstances?" Lady Carmichael asked, sounding a little surprised though Rachel caught the way that the Duke's eyebrows fell low over his eyes. "I am sorry to hear that. Might I ask what happened?"

Silence fell around the room and Rachel closed her eyes, her face growing hot with embarrassment. Her mother ought not to have asked that question. It was not something that even ought to be considered and yet, Lady Carmichael had spoken of it without even a seeming moment of hesitation. Rachel did not know what to do or what to say as the silence began to overpower the room.

"I think we must take our leave."

Rachel's eyes shot open as the Duke of Longford got to his feet, leaving his full tea cup sitting on the table in front of him.

"Chiddick?" His gaze once more swept the room. "Thank you for your company. Good afternoon."

Without so much as another word and without waiting to see if his cousin would follow him, the Duke of Longford marched to the other end of the room, opened the door and stepped out. Rachel rose to her feet, as did her mother and sister, though it was now much too late.

"I *do* apologise for our hasty departure." Lord Chiddick too got to his feet, though his face was a little flushed. "Thank you for your company and for the tea." With a bow, he opened his mouth to say something more, seemed to think better of it and then made his way from the room.

Rachel sank back down into her chair, looking at no-one in particular and finding herself quite astonished by all that had just taken place.

"Goodness," Lady Carmichael murmured, herself resuming her seat. "I do not know what to make of that."

"It is quite clear that the Duke of Longford is a gentleman who cares very little for the thoughts or the attention of others," Bettina stated, sending a sharp look towards Rachel. "He hardly spoke to anyone and then left incredibly abruptly – which is the most displeasing thing. You had asked him a perfectly decent question, Mama, and then he left without even considering them – without even considering you!"

"It may be that he did not want to answer," Rachel replied, feeling the urge to come to the Duke's defense. "It was a rather personal question and –"

"He did not need to be so abrupt!" Bettina exclaimed, interrupting Rachel. "That was utterly disgraceful. I cannot imagine what made him think he could behave in such a way."

"He is a Duke," Lady Carmichael sighed, shaking her head. "I suppose, in that way, he is very well used to doing what he pleases without much consideration to others."

Rachel closed her mouth and chose not to say anything further. There was truth in what her mother said, she considered, for the Duke of Longford *had* been rather rude in the way that he had walked away from them all and in saying nothing to her mother but, at the same time, she recognized that there had been a rudeness in her own mother's manner in pursuing what was, she was sure, a very tender subject for the Duke.

Frowning, Rachel sat back in her chair, her tea cup in her hand. Despite her mother's rudeness and the comments made by her sister, Rachel had to admit that she was wondering exactly what it was that had made the Duke hurry away from them all in such an abrupt manner. What was it about his father's passing that had been so troubling? And why was it that his cousin was willing to speak of it but the Duke was not?

Chapter Ten

"You ought not to have spoken of it."

Andrew scowled as Lord Chiddick frowned. "I am sorry, cousin, but I did not – "

"You did not *think*!" Andrew exclaimed, the carriage rattling over the cobbles. "That was not something I would ever disclose to anyone and certainly not to the three ladies present there!"

Lord Chiddick lifted an eyebrow. "Not even to Miss Grifford?"

Andrew shook his head. "Certainly not."

"Why not?"

A frown pulled at Andrew's forehead. "Why should I tell Miss Grifford about it?"

"Because you are rather attached to her, are you not?"

Andrew blinked rapidly and then laughed, shaking his head despite the way his heart twisted within him. "Certainly, I am not."

"Are you quite certain?" His cousin lifted one eyebrow as Andrew turned his head to look out of the window. "I thought you danced with her twice last evening and the second one was the waltz!"

"I did, yes, but that is not because I had any sort of specific feelings as regards the lady," Andrew replied, firmly. "It is only because I felt myself obliged towards her. I will not go into the reasons as to why that is but no, you can be assured that there was nothing of import on my part as regards her."

"Oh." Lord Chiddick frowned heavily as Andrew glanced back towards him. "Then why did you wish to call upon her?"

"*I* did not," Andrew emphasized, though he found himself growing a little hot as he recalled the conversation. "You stated that you should like to call upon Miss Grifford and, given that you were not acquainted with her mother or her sister, I offered to come with you in order to make the correct introductions."

There was a brief silence, only for Lord Chiddick to harrumph, perhaps not quite believing that Andrew was speaking the truth. Andrew did not care to explain any further, letting himself sigh gently as he closed his eyes and sat back.

"You will not dance with her at the ball tomorrow evening, then?"

Andrew cracked open one eye and saw his cousin's lifted eyebrow. "I am not inclined towards dancing," he stated, "as you well know."

"Ah, but that is not what I asked you." Lord Chiddick's smile began to grow again. "I asked if you would choose not to dance with the lady again."

"If I am disinclined towards dancing, then I am quite sure that I will be disinclined towards dancing with Miss Grifford." It was the only answer he could give and yet, as he spoke those words, they did not satisfy him. He felt as though he were deliberately betraying himself, pretending that he did not have an interest in the lady when the truth was, there was something flickering there which he was entirely uncertain about. With another sigh, he closed his eyes again and remained silent for the rest of the journey home, doing all he could to keep his mind away from Miss Grifford.

"You have a letter, Your Grace."

Andrew, who had called for the butler to enter, took it from the silver tray the butler held out to him. "I thank you."

"Is there anything else?"

Glancing to Lord Wrexham – who then shook his head – Andrew dismissed the butler and then looked at the letter.

"Please, do not refrain on my account!" Lord Wrexham waved a hand. "If it is of any importance, then – "

"It probably will be nothing of importance," Andrew replied, turning the letter over though he immediately frowned. "However, there is no seal here."

"No seal?"

Andrew shook his head. "There is wax to close the letter, yes, but there is no seal pressed into it. That is a little unusual."

"Indeed." Lord Wrexham ran one hand over his chin and then shook his head. "Perhaps a bill of some sort."

"Mayhap." Andrew broke the wax, unfolded the letter and then read the few lines. His eyes widened, his heart beating furiously as he took in what was said, barely hearing Lord Wrexham asking what the problem was. He read it again, then with a shake of his head, looked across to his friend. "I can hardly believe what I have just read."

"Tell me." Lord Wrexham's eyes were rounded, clearly a little concerned over what Andrew had read. "Is it troubling?"

Andrew nodded. "Very." Clearing his throat, he held the letter out again. "'Your Grace, I write with grave concern for your welfare. Please be very cautious and careful in your day to day goings-on. There is someone who means you harm.'"

Lord Wrexham's eyes widened. "Is that all it says?"

"Yes."

"Good gracious." Lord Wrexham shook his head. "Whatever does that mean?"

"I do not know."

"And no-one has signed it?"

Andrew shook his head. "No, there is no signature here. And with no seal in the wax, it is impossible to determine who wrote it."

Lord Wrexham rubbed his chin. "And no knowledge as to where it came from? The butler would not have taken note?"

"I do not think so," Andrew replied, quietly. "I do not know what to make of it, I must confess."

His friend frowned. "Will you take it seriously?"

"I think I should, though I do not know who it is that would mean me harm. I have no enemies."

"Not that you know of, anyway."

Andrew's eyebrows lifted. "Do you mean to say that there are those in society who wish me harm?"

Lord Wrexham managed a small smile. "That is not what I meant. I do not know anyone, no, just as you do not. However, that is not to say that there is no-one in society who would wish you to be harmed. Perhaps someone is upset with your demeanour or –"

"Someone who would wish me grievous harm, though?" Andrew queried, frowning. "That does not make any particular sense. There would be a great disservice done to someone, I think, rather than someone who would think me disagreeable or the like. I have not upset anyone, I have not insulted anyone or the like. There must be something serious here that I am unaware of."

Lord Wrexham got up and then went to pour them both a little brandy, bringing a glass over to Andrew who accepted it without hesitation, grateful for his friend's consideration.

"Do you think that this might be related to your father's passing?"

Andrew frowned, his heart slamming against his ribs for a moment. "What do you mean?"

"I mean simply that. I wonder if this is related to the passing of your father. After all, if you were concerned that your father's situation was not natural, that there was something untoward about it, then could it not be that whoever thought to harm your father might now seek to harm you?"

Considering this, Andrew shook his head. "I do not know. I am still uncertain as to whether or not my father's accident – the accident which led to his death – has any true darkness. It might just have been an accident."

"But you are not entirely convinced either way."

Andrew shook his head.

"But then surely my suggestion is a good one," his friend continued, before taking a sip of his brandy.

"I cannot be sure of anything. Nor can I understand why whoever has written to me has done so without putting their name to the letter."

"Because they clearly wish to remain secret."

"But why? Why not put their name to the letter and tell me precisely who it is? What could be their purpose in standing back from such details? That would give me the very best warning, would it not? If they put their name to it then I would be able to understand who they were and their motivations for speaking to me about such things."

Lord Wrexham shook his head. "They must have their reasons."

"But what are those reasons?" Andrew questioned. "They have only given me confusion and doubt rather than clarity."

After a few moments, Lord Wrexham let out a small breath and then shook his head. "As I have said, they must have their reasons for being so particular and so cautious. My only question now is whether or not you will be willing to do as they have suggested."

Andrew frowned. "What do you mean?"

"Will you be cautious? Will you be careful? Will you be more cautious as you make your way through society?"

"I do not even know what I am to look for!" Andrew exclaimed, his brandy sloshing wildly in the glass. "How can I even know what to do?"

"I... I do not know precisely but perhaps you ought to consider all that has been said," his friend replied, slowly. "Look about you a little more. Be cautious as to who you befriend, who you speak to."

"Given that I speak to very few people, that will not be particularly difficult," Andrew replied, a little ruefully. "But yes, I will consider what has been written to me, of course. Someone has clearly got enough concern for my welfare so as to write to me."

"And perhaps has done so by placing themselves in danger," Lord Wrexham suggested, his brow furrowed. "Please be cautious, old friend. I should not like what happened to your father to happen to you also."

Andrew shook his head, quickly dismissing such a thing. "I do not think that anything akin to that will happen to me."

"Why do you not think so?" his friend replied, sharply. "You do not know what it is that this person means for you. Be careful, my friend. Be very careful indeed."

Chapter Eleven

Rachel was so very tired of hearing her mother and sister arguing that she wanted to return to her bedchamber, pull the covers over her head and block out the sound as best as she could.

Instead, she attempted to keep reading though she was not very successful. They were about to make their way to Lord and Lady Plockton's ball and though she was prepared and ready – albeit without her best gloves which, despite her best attempts to keep them to herself were now on Bettina's hands – her sister and her mother were still not present. Rachel did not know what it was that kept them. She was a little surprised that her mother was so willing to be tardy but mayhap it was Bettina's refusal that held them back.

I shall see the Duke of Longford tonight.

Rachel shook her head to dismiss the thought. It was nothing but foolishness and she recognized it as such. Her questions about the Duke and particularly about the quick way he had quit their company had continued to linger on in her mind until she had not been able to think of anything else. Every time the Duke of Longford came to her mind, however, she made sure to dismiss it just as quickly, for there was very little point in considering this gentleman. It would only hurt her heart to permit herself to continue thinking of him in such a way for she would never be given answers to her questions. Besides which, she knew very well why he had danced twice with her and it certainly was not because he wanted to pay her special attention. He had felt sorry for her, had felt his sympathy for her situation grow and thus, had decided to show her a little consideration. There was nothing more than that.

"Bettina!"

The door flew open and Bettina strode into the room, quickly followed by her mother.

"I want your pearls."

Rachel blinked. "I beg your pardon?"

"I want your pearls!" Bettina repeated, her voice rising in frustration. "Do you not understand? The pearls that you have threaded through your hair are to be mine. Now, please go and fetch the maid and –"

"I certainly shall not!" Rachel exclaimed, surprise slamming through her. "the maid spent an inordinate amount of time placing them in my hair and I will not waste more time in having them removed so they might go into yours! Besides which, you have your own adornments and they are quite suitable."

"But they are not the *pearls*!" Bettina shouted, her hands curling into fists and her foot stamping hard on the floor. "I want the pearls! They will suit me better and I *insist* that I am given them at once! Rachel does not require them. Rachel does not need them!" Her arms folded over her chest, her eyes narrowing, fixing themselves to Rachel. "And if I do not get them, then I will not be going to the ball."

Rachel sighed inwardly, fully expecting her mother to agree that this was just what Rachel ought to do, simply in order to keep the peace. The maid would be called, she would have to sit for another hour waiting for the pearls to be removed from her hair and then even longer for them to be threaded through Bettina's hair instead! Looking to her mother, she saw Lady Carmichael steady herself with a brief close of her eyes, only to say the most unexpected thing.

"Then, Bettina, you will not attend the ball."

Rachel's eyes flared in surprise, just as Bettina's hands fell back to her sides in clear astonishment.

"I am not about to insist that the maid comes and does Rachel's hair all over again simply so that *you* might be given the pearls."

"But I want them!"

"I am well aware of that," Lady Carmichael replied, grimly. "In fact, I believe the entire household is aware that you want the pearls but on this occasion, you are being quite ridiculous. We are already tardy because of the fuss you have made over this and your sister has already been forced into giving you her gloves! I grow weary of this, Bettina. Your sister is right in what she said to me and I have decided that it is going to come to an end. I will not continually give you preference, Bettina, simply because you demand it. Rachel must be considered too, even though she is the younger daughter. I hope I have made myself clear in this regard."

The joy in Rachel's heart was so great, she could barely contain it. She found herself smiling, despite the fact that Bettina let out a shriek of frustration and caught her mother's eye for just a moment.

Lady Carmichael smiled softly. "Come, Rachel," she said, gesturing to her to rise and set the book aside so they might make their way to the carriage. "It seems as though Bettina is to remain at home this evening."

"No, I will not!" Bettina screamed, the sound ricocheting around the room as she hurried after Rachel. This is entirely unfair, Mama. I *must* be given the pearls! I *demand* them!"

Lady Carmichael slipped her arm through Rachel's, pulling her a little closer than ever before. "I am sorry for the preference I have shown your sister," she said, softly. "Her voice can be a good deal louder than yours and my weariness has taken a hold of me on many an occasion."

"But not on this occasion?" Rachel asked, as her mother nodded.

"No, not on this occasion," Lady Carmichael replied, having to speak a little more loudly so as to be heard over Bettina's screaming. "And let this be the first occasion of many."

***

"I can hardly believe it!"

"I was quite astonished by it myself," Rachel laughed, her arm through Miss Renfrew's as they walked around the ballroom together. "I do believe my mother to be quite genuine, though she still does give Bettina preference... as can be seen in how she hurried Bettina over to speak to Lord Chiddick and did not notice when I stepped away."

"I do like Lord Chiddick," Miss Renfrew murmured, softly. "Though he is very... enthusiastic in everything."

Rachel smiled. "Yes, he is. And I have a suspicion that you prefer Lord Wrexham anyway."

Miss Renfrew did not respond to this with anything other than a small smile and Rachel chuckled softly.

"He has already signed your dance card," she continued, as though to prove to her friend that there was an interest on both sides. "And though he signed mine also, he appeared very eager indeed to write his name upon yours."

"He is very considerate," Miss Renfrew admitted, quietly. "Lord Chiddick was very considerate also, I must admit. He has signed both of our dance cards and was busy looking at Bettina's dance card when we took our leave."

Rachel considered this and then nodded. "Though I do not have any interest in furthering an acquaintance with Lord Chiddick," she said slowly, seeing Miss Renfrew frown. "He is an excellent gentleman, I am sure, but he is a little too fervent about everything for my considerations! Much too efficacious." She laughed and made to say more, only to catch the sight of something which made her frown. "Look." Nudging Miss Renfrew, she directed her gaze to a footman who, for whatever reason, was tipping a few drops of something into a glass of whiskey. "Whatever is he doing?"

Miss Renfrew frowned. "I do not know. That is rather unusual."

"Could it be something that has been requested by one of the gentlemen?" Rachel asked, wondering whether gentlemen possessed any items to augment their whiskey with an additional vigor. "Do they do such things?"

Miss Renfrew shook her head. "No, I do not think so."

"Perhaps we should follow." There was something about this situation, something about the covert way that the footman was now placing the vial back in his pocket and glancing about him, which gave Rachel a warning. "Just to be sure that there is nothing untoward taking place."

"That is certainly a good idea," Miss Renfrew agreed as they both began walking after the footman, seeing him weave this way and that. "It seems as though he has a purposeful destination."

"Yes, he does." Rachel frowned all the harder as she looked at her friend for a moment and then back to the footman. "I do not know what this is about but I am a little troubled."

They continued following the footman for some minutes, seeing him step to the back of the room and, upon following him there, saw him step closer to a gentleman whom Rachel recognized immediately.

"The Duke!"

The gentleman took the whisky from the footman without a word, barely glancing at him – and Rachel found herself hurrying forward, rushing towards the Duke as he brought the whiskey to his lips. She did not know what it was about what she had seen but for some reason, the words Lord Chiddick had said about the troubling passing of the Duke's father bit down hard into her mind.

She caught his arm but it was too late. He had taken a sip though, thankfully, not a big one. "Your Grace!"

The Duke spluttered, clearly stunned by her action and pulling out a handkerchief, coughed into it which, Rachel considered, was something of a relief if it meant that he had not drank yet more whiskey.

"Miss Grifford, whatever is the meaning of this?" he demanded, his face rather red as he stuffed his handkerchief back into his pocket and rounded on her. "I do not know what it is you think you are doing but –"

"Did you send the footman to fetch that whiskey for you?" she interrupted, relieved that the Duke of Longford was alone and therefore, had no-one who had witnessed her strange action. "Was he on hand when you asked for it?"

The Duke nodded, his gaze sliding towards Miss Renfrew before returning to her. "Yes."

"You cannot drink the rest," she said, firmly. "I saw – we both saw – the footman putting something from a small vial into your glass."

Rather than throw aside that idea as nonsense or laugh at her for it, the Duke of Longford's eyebrows lifted so very high, they almost hit his hairline. He did not say anything for some minutes, staring at her as though he was not certain that she had told him the truth and was searching her face for it.

"I witnessed it also," Miss Renfrew said, perhaps seeing what Rachel had seen in the Duke's face. "Though it was Rachel – that is, Miss Grifford – who insisted on following the footman to see where the drink was going."

"And when I saw it came to you, I found myself filled with a great concern, to the point that I acted as I did," Rachel explained, finding herself a little embarrassed at the astonishment in the Duke's face. "Perhaps I am entirely mistaken and it is something that you yourself requested that the man put in but – "

"I did not such thing." The Duke ran one hand down his face and then, turning, set the whiskey glass down on the table behind him. "I do not understand. Why would –"

He stopped short as though Rachel or Miss Renfrew had interrupted him, only for his face to go very white indeed. Rachel found herself stepping closer, one hand going to his arm as she worried he might suddenly topple forward, only for the Duke of Longford to shake his head and then clear his throat.

"Thank you, Miss Grifford." He put one hand to hers and, lifting it, bowed over it. "You have done me a great service. I confess I do not know what it is that was placed in here but given that I am feeling a trifle unwell now – no doubt from whatever was in that concoction – I have been saved from a very painful experience."

"You are unwell?" Rachel found her hand tightening on his though he did not pull it away and she did not step back. "Your Grace, might I call someone for you? Or send for your carriage? Or for the doctor?"

The Duke shook his head. "I will be quite all right, I am sure. It is only a small feeling of illness, which, as I have said, must be solely down to your willingness to aid me. Thank you, Miss Grifford." A small smile lifted the corner of his mouth. "Might I ask if you would be willing to consider a dance? And you also, Miss Renfrew?"

Rachel blinked in surprise and quickly released his hand. "You said a moment ago that you were feeling a trifle unwell."

"But it is not enough to push me from the ball. I presume that whoever attempted to do such a thing was hopeful that I would quit the ballroom and return home and I should like to prove to them that they have been entirely *un*successful, if you gather my meaning?"

Rachel exchanged a glance with Miss Renfrew who, after a moment, shrugged both shoulders and then smiled.

"I should be glad to," she said, handing her dance card to the Duke. "Though so long as it is not because you feel obliged, Your Grace. Miss Grifford did not do this in order to secure a dance!"

"I am very well aware of that," came the quick reply, though Rachel noticed how the gentleman's smile grew rather than faded. "That would be a most extraordinary thing to do." That smile and his dark eyes flicked towards Rachel and for a moment, she saw him in an entirely new light. He was not frowning, his expression was not shadowed and the way he looked at her brought a lightness and a brightness to her heart which she had not felt before. When it came time to hand him her dance card, their fingers brushed and Rachel jumped in surprise, the touch making her skin burn as the heat in her fingers rushed up her arm.

It was all very strange.

"Oh, I must take my leave in search of Lord Rushford!" Miss Renfrew, hearing the next dance announced, turned quickly and hurried away, leaving Rachel and the Duke standing alone together – something which Rachel knew ought not to be done. She blinked, glanced at the Duke and then took her dance card back from him with a murmur of thanks.

"The country dance this time, Miss Grifford, though I should like to waltz with you again on another occasion," he said, his eyes alive with a sudden interest as he gazed back at her. "I did enjoy our dance."

"As did I," Rachel admitted, quietly, not quite certain where to look. "Might I ask you something, Your Grace?" She looked up at him, just as his gaze turned to the whiskey he had left on the table.

"After what you have just done for me, Miss Grifford, I believe you can ask me anything."

She nodded, pressed her lips tight together as she considered and then nodded half to herself, filling herself with the courage she needed to ask this rather probing question. "Is there someone trying to harm you? Is that why the footman did such a thing?"

The Duke let out a small sigh and then shook his head. "I do not know, Miss Grifford. I confess that I am rather astonished at all of this, though it is not unexpected."

Rachel's eyes flew wide. "Not unexpected? What can you mean by that?"

There was another pause and then the Duke shrugged as though inwardly considering whether or not he ought to tell her this. "I have had a very strange note today, Miss Grifford. A note which has warned me that there is someone amongst society who wishes me harm." He passed one hand over his eyes as Rachel caught her breath, both astonished and horrified to hear this from him. "I do not know why I am telling you this. Perhaps it is because of what you have done for me... I do not know. However," he continued, looking back at her, "it seems that this whiskey, this *poisoned* whiskey is proof that this letter I received, this warning, is quite true. And I am now rather worried."

"Who would wish you harm?" she found herself saying, words tumbling over each other. "I will not pretend that you are the most jovial of gentlemen but there can surely be nothing within you that would prompt such dark actions?"

The Duke looked at her and then chuckled, making Rachel's eyes widen all the more. She did not understand why he laughed, not at such a time as this, though after a moment, he gave her the explanation.

"You are very honest indeed, Miss Grifford and in truth, I find that quite refreshing," he told her, still smiling. "Yes, I am not the most jovial gentleman in all of London but yes, at the same time, I have done nothing which would bring about such a desire within someone else. I cannot understand it. That is why you find me both troubled and confused, Miss Grifford, for that is precisely what this letter *and* this whiskey have brought me. Confusion. Doubt. Uncertainty. And now, worry."

Rachel nodded slowly, then lifted her shoulders and let them drop. "Should I be able to be of any use to you, Your Grace, in aiding you in this matter then you have my willingness." Her smile grew wry. "My mother is attempting to improve things between my sister and myself and in how we are treated but I can assure you, I will still be very much unnoticed at occasions such as this – though mayhap that will be to an advantage in such situations as this."

The Duke offered her a small, wry smile. "That is very generous of you, Miss Grifford. I would be foolish to refuse, I think, given what has just now taken place."

Rachel's eyes flared in surprise, having expected the Duke to refuse her.

"But you must not disadvantage yourself," he continued, quickly. "Do not do anything for my sake only. It would not be right."

Rachel nodded, finding herself considering the gentleman for a moment as their eyes met. There was a gentleness to him which she had not expected, a softness about his eyes and a hint of tenderness in his smile which seemed quite at odds with the dark demeanor she knew him to carry. There seemed to be nothing further for the two of them to say and, with a small smile, she turned away, ready to go in search of her mother and sister again.

"Ah, there you are, Rachel."

Coming face to face with her mother, Rachel attempted to stammer an answer, seeing how her mother's gaze went over Rachel's shoulder to where the Duke of Longford was standing.

"Good evening, Your Grace," Lady Carmichael said, a little more loudly than Rachel thought she needed to. "I do apologise if I interrupted your conversation but my daughter is unchaperoned, as you can see and does not even have her friend with her!"

"Miss Renfrew went to dance," Rachel replied quickly, not wanting her mother to start making connections were there were none. "And I was just about to come in search of you."

"That is just as well," came the slightly sharp reply, "for it is entirely improper for a young lady such as yourself to be standing talking to a gentleman without a chaperone."

"I was seeking Miss Grifford's dance card, which I ought to have done whilst she was in company, of course," the Duke interrupted. "I must apologise for my oversight. I am afraid that I am often quite taken up with my own thoughts and expectations in matters such as these and quite forget about propriety and the like."

"I see." Lady Carmichael did not sound in the least bit convinced, though she did smile at least. "And have you signed her dance card, Your Grace?"

"Yes," the Duke confirmed, nodding to both Rachel and then to her mother. "Forgive me, Lady Carmichael, for my lack of consideration. I will make certain to be more careful in the future."

Rachel's relief grew as her mother managed a small smile, glad that she was not about to be in any particular difficulty over this mistake.

"But of course, Your Grace," Lady Carmichael said, reaching out to take Rachel's hand. "Now, do excuse us. I must return to my other daughter now."

Letting herself be led away, Rachel chose to say nothing and instead waited for her mother to speak. With a glance or two in her direction, upon catching her mother's eye, Rachel managed to give her a smile but nothing more.

"I must ask if there is any sort of connection between the Duke of Longford and yourself," Lady Carmichael asked, her eyebrows knotting together just a little. "You have been often in conversation with him from what I can see *and* he did come to call upon you."

"He hasn't come to call on me, Mama," Rachel replied, quickly. "It was Lord Chiddick who wished to be introduced to Bettina and to yourself and being Lord Chiddick's cousin, the Duke obliged him. That is all."

"And the dancing and conversation?"

Rachel shook her head gently and looked away from her mother's considered gaze. "He is a quiet gentleman, Mama. His dances are unexpected but they are not also solely for me alone. He is also to dance with Miss Renfrew."

"But he has danced a little more with you and *one* of them was the waltz."

"Do not think anything of it, Mama, I beg you," Rachel pleaded, seeing the flicker of hope in her mother's eyes. "Besides, do you not think that the Duke of Longford has a heavy, shadowy demeanour about him? That there is a heaviness to him which is most difficult?"

Lady Carmichael considered this and then let out a light, tinkling laugh and swept her arm through Rachel's. "I will not pretend it is not just as you have said but all the same, if there was a genuine interest there, if there was something quite wonderful between the two of you then I would not protest for all the world!"

"Well, there is not," Rachel stated, firmly. "Thank you, Mama, but there is nothing other than a mere acquaintance between the Duke of Longford and I... and that is, I am sure, all that there shall ever be."

Chapter Twelve

"There is something untoward going on."

Andrew barely noticed the way his friend jumped out of this chair in evident surprise as he sailed into the room, such was his determination to speak.

"Whatever is the matter?" Lord Wrexham's eyes were filled with surprise as Andrew began to pace up and down the room. "Has something happened?"

"Yes. No." Andrew paused and then rubbed one hand over his face. "Almost."

"Something *almost* happened?"

Andrew nodded. "Yes. That is it."

His friend frowned. "What was it?"

"Miss Grifford."

Lord Wrexham blinked. "You mean to say that Miss Grifford is the one who came to injure you? That she – "

"No, no, not in the least," Andrew interrupted, quickly. "She prevented me from being injured for which I am very grateful."

"I do not understand." Lord Wrexham passed one hand over his eyes as Andrew tried his best to explain.

"Miss Grifford spied a footman dripping something from a vial into the whiskey I had ordered. She did not know it was mine, of course, and therefore followed it just to see where it was taken. I believe she had an inkling that something was wrong. When I took it from the footman, she practically knocked it from my hand, though not before I had taken a small sip."

Lord Wrexham's eyes rounded. "Goodness. What was in the vial?"

"I do not know."

"But you believe it was poisoned?"

Andrew nodded slowly. "I believe that there was something in it which ought not to have been. Though I only imbibed a little, my stomach did cramp severely and when I returned home, I was in something of a sweat."

"Though you danced."

"Yes, I did, but that was simply because I was determined to dance and not return home. I wanted whoever had done such a thing to see that they had not succeeded in whatever it was they intended for me."

"That was bold."

"It was daring, yes, but I did it regardless." Andrew shrugged. "Thereafter, I stepped back and observed but I could see no-one sending any careful looks in my direction, wondering why I was not lying injured on the floor or some such thing. So I could make no guesses as to who the culprit might be."

"Mayhap they too were watching the footman and the whiskey," Lord Wrexham observed. "Mayhap they saw Miss Grifford grasping your arm and throwing it from your hand. Mayhap they saw that you did not drink it."

"Mayhap." Andrew shook his head. "All the same, it does not give me any answer as to who it was that did this. I cannot imagine why someone would want to poison my whiskey or why someone would want to injure me at all! I do not understand in the least."

"But it is clear that the note you received was speaking the truth," Lord Wrexham said, walking across the room and then turning back to face Andrew, his expression dark and one hand at his chin. "Someone *is* seeking to injure you. You might not know their motivations for that, at least, it was not given but there is clearly something about you which troubles them a great deal."

"To the point of wanting to remove me from this earth?"

Lord Wrexham shrugged. "That might not be what they are doing."

"But that *is* their intention. They want to harm me."

"But they might not want to kill you."

Andrew blew out a long, slow breath. "If this person – or persons – are the same who injured my father then I have every expectation that they are attempting to do the very same to me."

"That might well be so. However, what is it that you can do about it? How are you going to keep yourself safe and protected when you do not know who it is that is attempting to attack you?"

"I... " Andrew opened his mouth and then closed it again before frowning. "I do not know." His eyebrows lifted. "That is why I came to you. I had to tell someone in the hope of gaining some advice and since I am certain it cannot be *you* who is trying to injure me, I thought you would be the very best person to speak with."

A flicker of a smile crossed Lord Wrexham's face. "I am relieved that you do not think it is I who is trying to harm you," he said with a chuckle. "I can assure you, I am certainly doing nothing of the sort for I have no reason to do any such thing as that!"

Andrew managed a smile. "Thank you."

"So what is it that you are going to do?"

"I do not know. I – I should tell you that I spoke to Miss Grifford about all of this and she did offer to be of aid to me."

Lord Wrexham blinked, his expression a little fixed. "You spoke to Miss Grifford?"

"Yes."

"And she offered to be of assistance to you?"

Andrew nodded. "That is what I said, yes."

"I do not understand. What can she do for you?"

A hint of sadness tugged at Andrew's heart and he let out a slow breath. "I confess that I do not know but she suggested that, since she is easily able to move amongst society without being observed thanks to her mother's lack of interest in her – something that I find displeasing, of course – she might then be able to continue with her observations. I have told her all about the letter as I did not see a reason to keep it from her."

"Goodness." Lord Wrexham's eyes widened in obvious surprise. "I did not think... that is to say, I had not expected that you would be so willing to speak with her about such a thing as that. You do not know the lady very well."

Considering this, Andrew nodded slowly and then let out a small sigh as he thought about the lady for a few moments. "I believe I know her well enough to trust her. After all, it is not as though *she* is going to be doing anything to harm me, is she?" He laughed at this but saw his friend's expression remain exactly the same, clearly a little astonished that Andrew had chosen to be so open with the lady. "Besides," Andrew continued, in an attempt to do his best to explain himself as to why he had done such a thing as regards the lady, "she was the one who did her best to stop me from becoming injured. I felt it right to explain everything to her thereafter."

"I see."

"She is very generous to offer to aid me," Andrew finished, finding himself smiling briefly at the way Lady Carmichael had come in search of her daughter – though it had been much too late for the conversation had already taken place. "It would be unwise not to accept her kindness, I think."

"Then we should all meet together," Lord Wrexham stated, making Andrew's eyebrows lift in surprise. "We should all talk about what has taken place, what we think it all might be about and what we are to do next. Do you not think so?"

"I..." Andrew trailed off, finding the thought of pulling Miss Grifford into such a serious conversation to be a little unsettling. But, he considered, if he truly was to protect himself, then this might be the very best way to do it. "Very well. I will call on her and see if such a thing can be arranged."

"Capital." Lord Wrexham tilted his head. "The sooner, the better I should imagine. Though you will have to make a pretense to her mother as to why you are calling upon her, will you not?"

Andrew frowned. "What do you mean?"

"Simply that you cannot call on the young lady with the intention of talking to her about this matter without first disguising it as something else. You will have to suggest walking with her in the park or some such thing, for you will not be able to speak to her privately otherwise." Lord Wrexham chuckled as Andrew frowned. "Do you truly not understand what it is that I am saying?"

Slowly, understanding came to him and Andrew's frown deepened. "You mean to suggest that I will have to pretend to be intrigued in the lady. That I will have to make a pretense of calling upon her rather than simply seeking her company to talk about this matter at hand."

"Yes, that is precisely what I mean. Otherwise, how else will you be able to speak with her? It is not as though her mother is going to be able to listen in to a conversation about the note you have received and the strange vial placed into your whiskey, is she?"

Andrew hesitated, then closed his eyes. "I see what you mean. Yes, very well, I will pretend to have an interest in the lady. Though I will have to make it very clear to Miss Grifford as to why I am saying such things."

Lord Wrexham chuckled. "Or you could simply enjoy her company and see what comes of it?"

"No." Andrew cut the air with his hand, his brow furrowing all the more as the smile on his friend's face faded. "No, I will do nothing of the sort. Miss Grifford will know all and I hope she will be contented with it."

"Let us hope that *you* will be contented with it also," Lord Wrexham replied, a slight glint in his eye. "For I am quietly suspicious that, in a short while, you may find yourself very confused indeed."

***

"Miss Grifford." Andrew cleared his throat and tried to smile, fully aware that three sets of eyes were fixed to him.

"Yes, Your Grace?" Miss Rachel Grifford's eyes were slightly wider than usual, a gentle pink in her cheeks which, Andrew had to admit, did make her appear rather beautiful.

But he could not let thoughts like that distract him.

"I was hopeful that... " Hearing a slight hitch of breath, he turned his attention to Miss Bettina Grifford, seeing the way her eyes rounded and her face, instead of holding any color, went very pale indeed.

"Yes, Your Grace?" Lady Carmichael spoke with a firmness which redirected his attention back towards Miss Rachel Grifford and, clearing his throat, he gave a small nod.

"Yes, of course. My apologies." Clasping his hands in his lap and wondering at the tension which knotted his stomach and ran up his spine, he let out a slow breath and then forced a smile. "Miss Grifford, I was hopeful that you might be willing to walk with me in the park tomorrow."

There was another gasp though it was, again, from Miss Bettina Grifford rather than from her sister. Miss Rachel Grifford's eyes rounded and she stared at him as though he had quite lost his mind in asking her such a thing.

"Miss Grifford?" Andrew asked again, only for Lady Carmichael to let out a squeak which, when he looked at her, sent a flush rising up into her cheeks.

"My daughter accepts, of course!" she exclaimed, rising to her feet and hurrying across to Miss Rachel Grifford, grasping her hand and patting it furiously with the other. "Is that not so, Rachel?"

She blinked and then nodded slowly. "Yes, I suppose it is."

"That is not particularly enthusiastic, Rachel." Miss Bettina Grifford spoke up, her tone rather icy. "You are not showing any delight in the Duke's request and seem to have no genuine interest in furthering an acquaintance with him!"

Andrew frowned immediately, sending a sharp look to Miss Bettina Grifford though when she caught his eye, she merely smiled rather than appearing at all embarrassed by his response.

"I am a little overwhelmed, that is all." Miss Rachel Grifford spoke again, her voice very soft indeed though her eyes returned to his face rather than looking at her sister. "You are very generous, Your Grace."

"Not in the least. It would be an honour," he replied truthfully, while at the same time, silently praying that she would understand what he meant by such a request. "Might we say tomorrow afternoon, then? I can come here in my carriage and thereafter, we might go together to the park? With your chaperone, of course."

"How *very* generous, Your Grace!" Lady Carmichael exclaimed, while her daughter managed a vague nod. "I will make certain that we are both readily prepared. I will accompany her of course, but when you are walking, I will make certain to stay a few steps back. I do hope that will be suitable."

"I can make no protest," he replied, seeing her nod and smile. "I shall take my leave of you all now. I look forward to seeing you tomorrow, Miss Grifford."

As Andrew rose to his feet to take his leave, he found himself rather surprised that, though he had spoken of looking forward to seeing the lady again without any real thought of it, that was the truth which sank deeply into his heart. He *was* looking forward to being in her company again, *was* looking forward to having her in his carriage and walking with her.

How very strange indeed.

Chapter Thirteen

"It is most unfair."

Rachel attempted to hide the way she rolled her eyes but Bettina saw it nonetheless and immediately erupted into cries of anger and upset.

"It is not unfair," Lady Carmichael replied, ignoring the way that Bettina continued to protest. "The Duke of Longford wishes to walk with Rachel. Why then would you suggest that it is in any way unfair?"

"Because he ought to be considering me!" Bettina replied, her eyes red as though she was about to burst into tears. "I am the eldest and – "

"I am afraid that is not the way that such things work, my dear," Lady Carmichael replied, calmly. "I will admit to being rather surprised that the Duke would choose Rachel but that is something which he himself has decided."

Rachel frowned, her shoulders dropping as she took in her mother's words and found herself growing heavy-hearted over them. Even though her mother was being rather supportive in this connection with the Duke, she still found a way to upset Rachel even without meaning to.

Rachel swallowed hard and shook her head to herself before turning away to the front door, ready to receive the Duke's carriage.

"But you do not even like the Duke of Longford," Bettina protested again as Rachel listened without turning her head. "Is that not so, Mama? You said he was dark and beastly and – "

"And I still consider him so but given that he cares for your sister, what care I for that?" Lady Carmichael laughed, sending yet another dart into Rachel's heart. "He is a *Duke,* Bettina! And he wants to spend more time in your sister's company which might one day make her a Duchess! Can you imagine that?"

Rachel closed her eyes and said nothing. The Duke's request had come as a very great surprise but the more she had considered it, the more she had begun to wonder if the reason he had asked her for such a thing was because of what he had shared with her at the previous ball. If this was so that they might discuss matters in private, then that would be his reason for calling upon her and requesting such a thing, would it not? It would not be because he truly cared for her.

"The carriage, Mama."

Lady Carmichael let out a squeak of excitement, as though she was the one who would be walking with the Duke himself, and then caught Rachel's arm so they might descend the steps together – leaving a thoroughly frustrated Bettina behind.

"Your Grace." Rachel managed a smile as the Duke stepped out from the carriage to greet them. "Thank you for your prompt arrival."

"What a glorious day it is for our walk together," he said, smiling at her. "Please, permit me to assist you both into the carriage."

As was expected, the Duke first helped her mother into the carriage and thereafter, took her hand. What Rachel did not expect was for fire to erupt in her heart at the touch of his hand on hers, making her heart pound furiously. When she sat down in the carriage, Rachel did not know where to look, finding herself hot all over and embarrassed with it. Why should she have such a reaction to him? Despite her mother's excitement and her sister's frustration, Rachel was quite certain that the Duke had another motive for walking with her this afternoon, and permitting her heart to feel anything for him was stupidity indeed.

"It is a very fine afternoon, is it not?"

Rachel looked up at the Duke as they walked, glancing back over her shoulder to see her mother far enough away that the conversation would not be overheard.

"I believe that my mother will not hear us, Your Grace." Seeing the way his eyes flickered in confusion, she offered him a small smile. "I am quite sure there is another motivation behind this walk, Your Grace. You wanted to speak to me alone, did you not?"

The Duke of Longford's eyebrows knotted. "I suppose that is so. Though I am hopeful that we will still be able to enjoy a walk together, Miss Grifford."

"I am sure we shall, given the pleasant afternoon, but I would rather know what it is that you wanted to speak to me about," she said, firmly. "Is it to do with this note? And the whiskey?"

After a moment, the Duke nodded and Rachel's heart crumpled. She had been right in her thought that this was, then, only a pretense. There was no genuine interest in her company, no genuine desire for them to become more closely acquainted.

She sighed inwardly but then forced a smile. This was just what she ought to have expected.

"I spoke to Lord Wrexham about what happened," the Duke continued, quietly, clearly entirely unaware of the pain which now sliced through her heart. "He is a gentleman who knows my concerns over my father and – "

"Your father?" Rachel looked up at him sharply, recalling how Lord Chiddick had spoken of a troubling situation as regarded the late Duke. "Might I ask what you mean by that?"

There came a short pause, only for the Duke to nod as though he were confirming with himself that it was quite all right for him to do so. "My father died after falling from his horse. It did appear to be a tragic accident though, I am afraid, when I went to the scene where it had taken place, I found a red cloth tied to a stick only a few paces away from where my father's horse had reared up."

Fright captured Rachel's heart. "You mean to suggest that his horse was frightened into rearing up?"

"That has long been my suspicion," he admitted, quickly, "but I cannot confirm it. Nor can I understand who would do such a thing or why. My father was of excellent character, had no debts to anyone and from what I have learned about him since his passing, had no enemies to speak of either. There was nothing about him which spoke of darkness and I cannot imagine why someone would want to harm him in such a way."

"Perhaps this person did not mean for him to die."

The Duke frowned and immediately, Rachel flushed with embarrassment.

"I did not mean to speak out of turn. I do not know the situation and – "

"That is a good thought and not one that I have considered before now," the Duke interrupted, though he did not speak harshly. "I must admit that it would not make sense to me for I cannot find a single person who thought ill of him or who held anything against him. Therefore, I must believe that whoever did this did so in order to bring an end to his life – and that then makes me a little concerned that they are also going to be ending my life."

"Goodness."

"That is why I wish to do all I can to discover what is happening and who is doing it," the Duke continued, looking down at her. "And since you have offered to be of aid to me, I thought I should accept that offer though, in doing so, make you fully aware of all that has taken place thus far. It is rather concerning, is it not?"

"It is." Rachel paused for a moment in their walk, turning so she could look up at him carefully, seeing the worry in his eyes and finding herself wondering if this was the cause of his dark manner and demeanor. He carried a heavy burden, she realized, and that must trouble him a great deal.

"If you do not wish to continue being of aid to me, I quite understand," the Duke murmured, offering her his arm which she took without hesitation, walking alongside him again. "There is danger here, I fear and I certainly do not wish for you to put yourself at risk in any way."

"Oh, I have no intention of stepping back!" Rachel exclaimed, seeing his eyebrows lift in surprise at her exclamation. "Certainly not after you have told me about your late father and the burden you carry as regards that. That is truly dreadful, Your Grace. Yes, I should be very glad indeed to be of aid to you though aside from what I offered you, I do not know what else it is that I can do."

The Duke let out a slow breath and then, much to Rachel's surprise, smiled broadly. "Even hearing those words from your lips has given me a great encouragement," he told her, making Rachel smile back at him. "It has been difficult these last few years, knowing what I do about my father though they are only suspicions, I admit. Lord Wrexham has known of it but now... now it seems a good deal weightier."

"That is because it *is* weightier," she answered, gently. "You may be in danger. In truth, Your Grace, I believe that this confirms your concerns over your father."

"You do?"

Rachel nodded, pulling herself a little closer to him. "I believe that if this person is attempting to injure you, then there is every reason to believe that this same person did as you suspect as regards your father. There must be some correlation."

With another look towards her, the Duke blew out a long, slow breath and then nodded. "I find that I agree with you in that, Miss Grifford. Though... " Frowning, he looked away from her and then looked back again. "I think I must ask you for another favour, however. I must ask you if you are able to accept my courtship."

Shock rifled up Rachel's spine as she turned her head and gazed up into the Duke's eyes, seeing his steady gaze. She took in a long breath, holding it tight in her chest for a moment before releasing it. "You desire to court me?"

"Yes."

Her heart glowed.

"But only because we will not be able to talk in this manner unless we present ourselves to the *ton* as a courting couple," he continued, shattering the heat which had built up in her heart. "It will be difficult, I understand, but Lord Wrexham has made it quite clear to me that this is the only way that such a thing can take place. We will not be able to talk together otherwise."

Rachel swallowed hard and then nodded slowly. "I see what you mean," she answered, even though her warm happiness had been quickly replaced with a cold disappointment. "Though you must see that other gentlemen will no longer be able to consider me if that should happen. You are asking a great deal of me, Your Grace. I presume the courtship will have to come to an end once certain things are discovered or revealed?"

The Duke nodded. "Though I shall permit you to decide whether you are the one who ends our courtship or I should do so," he said, smiling as though he were offering her a great and valuable gift. "I think that would be fair."

Rachel wanted to say yes, the words were on the very tip of her tongue but she could not bring herself to do so. Though she understood why the Duke was suggesting this, though she agreed that it was the only way that society would permit them to be a little closer in company, she found herself hesitating for the sake of her own heart. To agree, to accept would mean that she would be pulled away from any potential happiness with any other gentleman and the ending of their courtship would be another difficulty also.

"Might I think on it?"

The Duke's eyebrows lifted in evident surprise at her request but, clearing his throat, he nodded. "Yes, of course. I understand that it is something of a consideration."

"It is," Rachel admitted, quietly. "You understand that it is not because I do not wish to be of aid to you or that I desire to step back from what I offered. Rather, it is because I must consider my own standing in society."

"Of course." The Duke managed a smile but it did not light his eyes. "I quite understand, Miss Grifford. Whatever you decide, I will be happy to accept."

Rachel smiled back at him and then looked away again, an uneasy silence growing between them. She was not certain what else to say, wondering if the Duke of Longford had expected her to agree without hesitation. There was much for her to consider and, truth be told, Rachel was entirely unsure as to what the right decision would be.

Her heart was crying out for her to say yes, to permit the Duke of Longford to court her but her mind was fighting back, reminding her that she would be ill considered by the *ton* should she do so and their courtship came to an end. To have feelings for the Duke of Longford was entirely unsuitable and yet, her heart would not pretend otherwise. She wanted to be closer to the Duke of Longford, wanted to draw near to him and to have his full attention... but at what cost?

***

"Good evening, Miss Grifford."

Rachel turned her head and smiled as Lord Wrexham came towards her. "Good evening, Lord Wrexham. I do hope you are enjoying the soiree?"

He nodded. "I am. Though I am disappointed there is no dancing this evening."

Rachel smiled gently. "Lord Chiddick expressed the very same thing," she replied, making Lord Wrexham's eyebrows lift. "He was speaking with me only a short while ago."

"Then he and I feel the very same way," Lord Wrexham replied, with a smile. "I prefer a ball rather than a soiree, I must admit. But soirees do give greater opportunity for conversation, I suppose."

"That is true," Rachel smiled, only for Lord Wrexham to glance to one side and then to the next before stepping closer and then much to Rachel's surprise, taking a small step closer. Her mother, father and sister were already stepped away from her – her mother and Bettina only a few steps away, however – but Lord Wrexham was clearly eager to talk to her privately.

"I hear you spoke with the Duke yesterday."

Rachel nodded, surprise catching her as she did so.

"Please do not think me forward, but I wanted very much to speak with you about the matter myself," Lord Wrexham continued, his voice a little lower now as she looked back at him. "As you may be aware, the Duke of Longford has brought me into his confidence as regards the matter with his father and also as regards the note he received of late."

Rachel nodded. "Yes, he informed of that."

"It was I who suggested that he offer a courtship," Lord Wrexham continued as a flush crept into Rachel's cheeks. "It would not be right for him to offer you so much attention without doing such a thing as that."

"Thank you for that suggestion," Rachel replied, wondering silently why he was telling her such a thing as that. "It was very considerate of you."

"But you have not accepted it?"

Rachel blinked.

"The Duke informed me of it," Lord Wrexham explained, as though he knew exactly what Rachel was thinking. "He was very matter of fact and explained all to me most succinctly. I can understand your reasons for wanting to be careful and cautious as regards you accepting the Duke's courtship but there is something that he did not speak of which I feel I must express to you now."

A little surprised, Rachel spread out both hands either side. "Please. Do tell me whatever it is you wish."

Lord Wrexham smiled. "I thank you. I should say that the Duke has not given me permission to say this to you – though he has not refused permission either – and therefore, he may be a little frustrated should you tell him of what I have said. Though I do not think that you shall."

A curl of curiosity ran up through Rachel's frame and she nodded slowly. "Very well."

"Capital." Lord Wrexham replied. "Now, the reason that I tell you this is because I believe that there could be potential for an excellent match between the Duke of Longford and yourself. I understand that he has told you that there will be no furthering of your connection beyond courtship and that even that will be brought to an end once matters with his safety are resolved but in saying that, the Duke himself ignores the possibility that he might find himself drawn to you and, thereafter, eager for your connection to continue."

Rachel's eyes flared wide, one hand clenching into a fist as she fought to contain her emotions. Hope had leapt to life, making her heart sing but she forced it back down, attempting to understand what Lord Wrexham meant.

"He may very well find himself caring for you." Lord Wrexham folded his arms across his chest. "He does not want to admit it, of course, for he has determined that he shall never permit himself to have any affection for any young lady simply because of the darkness in his past."

"You mean to speak of his father?"

Lord Wrexham nodded. "But he is talking to *you* about such things and I am quite convinced that, once the culprit is exposed, the Duke will realise all that he feels for you and, in that regard, will silently determine to move forward rather than back."

Rachel closed her eyes briefly, taking in a long, slow breath so that she might bring a little clarity to her thoughts. "I see."

"The Duke is a good man, albeit with a shadowy demeanour," Lord Wrexham finished, a little more gently than before. "I have known him for many years and I have seen how altered he has become ever since the passing of his father. I should like to see him restored to his former self, Miss Grifford, for he is not as he once was. I can assure you that, should such a thing occur, you would find him an excellent gentleman."

"I already do," Rachel replied, speaking a little more quickly than she had meant. "That is… "

Blushing, she dropped her head and closed her eyes again, only to hear Lord Wrexham chuckle softly.

"I understand precisely and I am glad to hear it. I do hope that you have not thought ill of me for coming to speak to you so boldly, Miss Grifford. I want what is best for my friend and, in all truth, I believe that you also are in need of some kindness. To my mind, this would be an excellent match for the both of you which is why I come to ask you to consider accepting the Duke's offer."

Rachel pressed her lips together, opened her eyes and then looked at Lord Wrexham again. "Thank you for being honest with me, Lord Wrexham. I do value what you have told me."

He smiled at her. "I am very glad to hear it. I shall take my leave of you now, before the Duke begins to wonder what it is that we are speaking of!"

Glancing across the room, Rachel caught the Duke's eye for a moment, having not seen him enter the soiree. A rush of heat ran through her and she swallowed hard before looking away. "Good evening, Lord Wrexham. You have given me a great deal to think on and I promise, I shall give it a great deal of consideration."

"I hope it is of benefit," he replied, inclining his head just a little. "Good evening, Miss Grifford."

Chapter Fourteen

Andrew eyed the glass of brandy which had been handed to him, a little uncertain as to whether or not he ought to drink it. He had been a good deal more cautious of late and even though the poisoned whiskey had been over a sennight ago, he still found his heart filled with nervousness every time he was given something to eat or drink at whatever occasion he attended.

"I watched that being poured myself," Lord Wrexham murmured, coming around to stand beside Andrew. "You need not worry. There is nothing in it."

"I thank you." Andrew took a sip and then let out a slow breath. "I am sorry I am so uncertain at times like these. After what happened – "

"I quite understand." Lord Wrexham smiled. "Might I ask if Miss Grifford has given you an answer as yet?"

Andrew's brow furrowed. "No, she has not. I confess that I did think she would give me her answer immediately and that she would not wait for such a long time considering."

"Oh?" Lord Wrexham arched any eyebrow and then chuckled. "Why should you think such a thing? Do you not think that the lady ought to consider all that might happen because of a connection between you, should there be one? After all, you are asking a great deal of her."

"Am I?" Andrew frowned. "I did not think it was all that significant. When the connection comes to an end – that is, after I have discovered who it is that has done such a thing and why – I will then be the one responsible for it in whatever way that Miss Grifford decides, and she will then be able to continue on, just as she pleases."

"But society will notice that and consider her a little.... affected because of it," Lord Wrexham explained, quietly. "She may not bear the blame but the *ton* will still whisper about her. She is also a young lady attempting to find a suitable match for herself, is she not? And in accepting your courtship – a courtship which she knows will soon come to an end, she is effectively ruining her chances of a successful Season. She will have to wait until next Season and, given how her mother and father treat her, can you be certain that she will be given that?"

Andrew rubbed one hand over his chin, sucking in a breath as he looked away. "I – in truth, I had not thought of such a thing as that."

"So you can see now why she is considering things," Lord Wrexham said, making Andrew nod. "She is a very considerate young lady to even be *thinking* of accepting such a thing for your sake. She will be giving up a great deal."

Clearing his throat, Andrew nodded again but said nothing, taking a sip of his whiskey and letting the sensation flood him. It was warm and it settled him a little, leaving him with a fresh understanding of Miss Grifford and all she was offering him in doing as she did. At the same time, bringing her to mind made his heart squeeze tight for a moment, leaving a broad smile to settle across his face though at the questioning look from Lord Wrexham, Andrew pushed it from his expression.

"Is she here this evening?"

"I do not know. I have not seen her as yet," Andrew answered, truthfully. "I have been keeping myself back from her so as not to put any pressure upon this decision."

"That is considerate of you." Lord Wrexham's expression grew to one of curiosity. "Have you no interest in going about here in search of her? If she is here, then would you not be able to speak with her? Even if it is just general conversation?"

Andrew shook his head, surprised at just how much he desired to do that very thing. It was as though he had been waiting for someone to make that suggestion in order for him to realize just how much he wanted to speak to Miss Grifford again. It had felt like a month between now and their last conversation, even though Andrew knew it had not been more than a few days.

"Are you sure?"

"Enough, my friend!" Andrew exclaimed, seeing his friend laugh. "Please, enough questions. I am quite able to speak to Miss Grifford myself whenever I should desire it. I do not think that I require your assistance with that."

"Your Grace? My lord?"

Andrew turned to see a footman holding a tray of delicacies. "Queen Currant Cakes!" he exclaimed, reaching for one. "They are one of my favourites." He took one from the tray and then bit into it, relishing the taste. "I have always enjoyed these, ever since I was a child."

"As have I," Lord Wrexham agreed, reaching out one hand for the cakes, only for the footman to turn abruptly and hurry away.

Lord Wrexham frowned. "How very odd. I am sure that – oh! Good gracious, stop!"

He smacked Andrew's hand so hard, the currant cake fell from Andrew's hand and threw itself towards the wall of the drawing room. Andrew made to demand to know what it was that his friend thought to be doing, only to realize that there was a warning in his friend's eyes.

"Why did that footman hurry away?" Lord Wrexham asked, coming closer and looking around the room. "He has left the room without going to another single person, even though there are at least ten others present. Why?"

Andrew swallowed hard. Was it just in his mind or was his throat feeling a little tighter than before?

"He came directly to you, with a tray filled with your favourite treats," Lord Wrexham pointed out. "And then he quickly hurried away, leaving no opportunity for any other to take one of the cakes. Does that not tell you something?"

The way his friend spoke sent worry shooting into Andrew's stomach. "It does."

"Are you feeling unwell?"

Andrew nodded, his stomach queasy. "I am. My stomach aches and my whole body feels hot."

"Then you should return home," Lord Wrexham stated, firmly. "We should have the doctor sent for and – "

"I do not want to." Pulling out his handkerchief, Andrew wiped at his forehead, aware of the sweat which had broken out. "It will prove to whoever is responsible that I have succumbed. I want to prove to them that they have not succeeded."

Lord Wrexham shook his head. "That is unwise. You need to recover."

"Who else is present this evening?" Andrew asked, ignoring his friend's concern. "I must take note of them all. The person responsible for this attempt at injuring me *must* be present."

His friend's eyes widened. "That is a good thought."

"Might I ask if everything is all right?"

Andrew turned around entirely, seeing his cousin standing there, a look of concern on his face. "Chiddick. I am quite all right. I was simply wondering who was present this evening." He forced a smile even though he did not feel it deep in his soul. He considered for a moment whether or not he ought to say something to his cousin, only to see the way Lord Wrexham shook his head. "It is an excellent soiree, is it not?"

His cousin nodded but he did not smile, that concern still lifting his expression. "Are you quite well? You do not look particularly – "

"I am quite well, I assure you," Andrew stated firmly, only to feel a sudden weakness wash over him. "I think that I – "

He did not say anything more, finding himself sinking to his knees and, as he did so, the whole world around him going black.

***

"Your Grace? Your Grace? Andrew?"

Andrew tried to open his eyes but found them too heavy. He tried to rub at them, tried to lift his hand but found he could not. There was too much weariness within him, too much fatigue that burned right through his whole body.

"You are awake, are you not?"

Andrew grunted and finally managed to crack open one eye, seeing the wide eyed expression of Lord Wrexham looking back at him. "What happened?"

"You fainted, cousin." Lord Chiddick was at his other side, leaning over what Andrew realized was a couch. "A little too much whiskey, mayhap?"

"Mayhap." Andrew finally managed to rub at his eyes and, after a moment, harnessed enough strength to push himself up. "My head aches."

"It could be from where you struck it against the floor," Lord Wrexham replied, quietly. "Can you stand?"

"My strength is returning," Andrew admitted, accepting a glass of water from his cousin with a grateful murmur. "I am sorry to have caused such an upset."

"The doctor was called," Lord Wrexham said, glancing to Lord Chiddick. "He has not yet arrived, however."

"I do not require a doctor," Andrew stated, firmly. "I am quite well. It was a faint, that is all. As my cousin has said, a little too much whiskey." He looked to his cousin. "Might you inform our host that I am well recovered and that the doctor does not need to be disturbed?"

Lord Chiddick nodded and then took his leave. Thereafter, Andrew rose to his feet, though he was forced to lean back and grasp the top of the couch given the way he wobbled.

"Steady, now, old friend," Lord Wrexham murmured, reaching out to put one hand on Andrew's shoulder. "It was the cake, I am sure."

"Yes, it must have been."

"I do not know what would have happened to you had you eaten all of it," Lord Wrexham continued, his hand slowly releasing from Andrew's shoulder. "That is the second time someone has attempted to injure you through what you eat or drink."

"But why?" Andrew closed his eyes as another wave of dizziness washed over him. "Again, I ask, why would someone do such a thing to me? I have no enemies. My father had no enemies. So what is it that they want from me?"

Lord Wrexham shrugged. "To teach you a lesson? To make you aware of what it is that you have done to them, even though, at the present moment, you can think of no-one?"

Andrew pinched the bridge of his nose and let out another breath. "I do not know. However, I realise now that I shall have to take a good deal more care than I have been, given what has happened."

"I would not accept any dinner invitations, certainly," Lord Wrexham agreed, speaking rather ruefully. "Not until we can understand why this is happening to you."

Andrew sat back down heavily rather than remaining standing. His stomach was still twisting this way and that, his heart was beating a little more quickly than usual and his mind was whirring with questions. Leaning forward, he put his elbows on his knees and dropped his head forward, taking in big gulps of air in the hope of ending the nauseous sensation pushing through him.

This evening was meant to have been one of enjoyment, not one of concern. And yet now, as he sat here and attempted to gather himself again, Andrew felt himself more troubled than ever.

Chapter Fifteen

"Father?" Rachel pushed open the door of her father's study, having already been granted permission to enter. "Might I speak with you?"

Her father looked up from his papers, quill in hand. "If you wish, though it cannot be for more than a few minutes. I have a good many matters to deal with."

"I understand." Licking her lips, Rachel clasped her hands lightly in front of her and took in a deep breath, looking up at her father and trying to steel her resolve. She had thought for a long time about the Duke of Longford's offer as regards their courtship and what it would mean and now, having come to a decision, she had to speak with her father.

"It is about the Duke of Longford."

That name had her father's head lifting sharply, his eyes fixed to hers, his astonishment more than apparent in his expression.

"I presume Mama has told you that the Duke has shown an interest in me of late?"

Lord Carmichael cleared his throat gruffly, frowning as he set his quill back in the jar. "She may have mentioned it in the passing but I was not certain that it was to be taken with any real seriousness."

Rachel's heart squeezed with the pain of her father's words but she did not let that pain push into her expression. "Yes, Father. There is a great deal of seriousness within the Duke's interest for he soon will come to seek your permission to court me."

Lord Carmichael's mouth dropped open and Rachel's face flamed with heat.

"Are... are you quite certain of this?"

She nodded. "I am."

"Are you sure of his interest?"

Again, she nodded, all the more embarrassed that her father did not believe her words. "The Duke of Longford and I took a walk some days ago and during that time, he stated very clearly that he wished to court me. I, however, have been considering it and have now given my attention to it. I have come to a decision."

"I... I see." Her father looked at her doubtfully, perhaps still disbelieving that all she said was true. "The Duke of Longford asked to court you and you have been considering your answer all this time?"

Rachel nodded.

"But why?" her father wanted to know. "I cannot understand you. If this is as you say, then why would you have to consider the Duke of Longford? I –"

"Is everything quite all right?"

Rachel turned her head to see her mother pushing open the door, a look of curiosity in her eyes. She groaned inwardly, having hoped that this conversation would have been kept from her mother for the time being until she was able to talk to the Duke of Longford himself.

"Yes, everything is quite all right," Lord Carmichael smiled, beckoning his wife in. "I must ask you something, my dear."

"Oh?" Lady Carmichael put one hand onto Rachel's arm. "What troubles you, Rachel? Why is it that you have come to your father?"

Rachel hesitated. "Mama, the Duke of Longford has asked to court me."

Lady Carmichael's hand tightened on Rachel's arm and she let out a squeak, one hand flying to her mouth, her eyes rounding.

"Can this be true, my dear?" Lord Carmichael asked, as Lady Carmichael blinked furiously. "Is this something that you have been aware of?"

"When?" Lady Carmichael whispered, drawing closer to Rachel as she held her arm in a vice-like grip. "When did he ask you this?"

Rachel hesitated, hoping that her mother would not be angry with her. "When we took a walk together in the park."

"What?" Lady Carmichael's hand loosened on Rachel's arm and she stepped back, the color draining from her face. "You did not tell me!"

"That is because she says she told the Duke she had to think about her answer," her father replied, making Lady Carmichael squeak an exclamation all over again. "Do you mean to tell me that this is true then, my dear?"

Rachel spread out her hands either side. "Mama, I wanted some time to consider it. What if the Duke and I do not suit? If the courtship comes to an end, then the *ton* will speak ill of me and –"

"But what if it does not come to an end?" Lady Carmichael interrupted, clearly ignoring her husband and instead, coming closer to Rachel again, staring into her face. "Do you not understand, Rachel? The *Duke* has asked to court you! You could be a Duchess! Why ever would you say that you required some time to consider? I do not understand it. I do not understand you! I cannot imagine why –"

"I will tell him my decision when I next speak with him, Mama," Rachel interrupted, having no desire whatsoever to have her mother criticize her. "He was very agreeable to my request for some time to consider. However, I wanted to inform my father before I spoke with the Duke of Longford, so that he would not be surprised when the Duke came to speak with him."

Lady Carmichael closed her eyes and let out a slow breath. "We must hope that you have not irritated him by your desire to *take your time*," she said, emphasizing the last few words. "He may decide that you are no longer the object of his interest because you have delayed so much. What if –"

"He will not, Mama," Rachel replied, firmly. "Now, if you are both quite contented, I shall write to the Duke this very afternoon and tell him that I should like to speak with him. Will that satisfy you both?" Finding a streak of anger breaking through her heart, she took in a deep breath and lifted her chin, looking at her father. "Will it be enough to convince you that I am speaking the truth?" She looked to her mother. "And will it satisfy you that he has *not* rejected me?"

Lady Carmichael blinked and then, much to Rachel's surprise, let out a squeal of excitement and threw her arms around her. "How delighted I am to hear it!" she cried, as Rachel swallowed her surprise. "Go! Write to the Duke at once and inform me – inform *us* – the moment you receive a reply."

Seeing the slightly curt nod from her father, Rachel took this as a sign to take her leave without saying anything more and, with a brief smile, she detached herself from her mother and walked out of the room. Her whole body was alive with a sudden anticipation, even though, as she reminded herself, she was accepting the offer of a courtship which had only one singular purpose.

And yet, there is hope, said a whisper in her heart as Lord Wrexham's words came to mind. *Perhaps, at the end of it all, I shall find myself a Duchess after all.*

***

"I was glad to receive your note."

Rachel glanced up at the Duke and then looked away again. "Thank you for agreeing to walk with me. I thought that, should we talk at my townhouse, my mother, sister and father would, no doubt, be quite determined to linger in the house and listen."

The Duke's eyebrows lifted though he said nothing. Instead, he simply offered her his arm which she took after a moment.

"I spoke to my father yesterday," Rachel continued, still not quite able to look at the Duke, still feeling tension ringing up her spine and sending a tremor into her heart. "Neither he nor my mother were aware of your request as regards courtship so I explained that to them. I – "

"You told them about everything?"

The Duke suddenly spun her around, staring down into her eyes as Rachel blinked in surprise, then shook her head.

"No, Your Grace," she said, softly. "No, of course I did not. You can trust me. I spoke to them only about your request for courtship. I would not dare to tell them a single thing about the difficulties and the dangers which have come upon you of late. That is not my place and I certainly would never dream of speaking them to anyone."

After a moment of searching her expression, the Duke of Longford seemed to relax. He nodded, closed his eyes and then offered her a small, wry smile.

"Forgive me," he said, quietly. "I ought not to have assumed that you would have done anything like that. That was my mistake."

"We are still learning about one another," Rachel replied, still speaking quietly and with as much gentle understanding as she could. "But I should like to assure you that you *can* trust me, Your Grace. I am not the sort of person who would ever dream of betraying a confidence. I would not whisper anything about you and your private matters to anyone, I can assure you of that."

"I see." The Duke smiled again and this time, it made the darkness in his expression lift. "Thank you, Miss Grifford, for that reassurance. I must apologise to you for my hasty response. It is not as though I have many people in my life whom I can trust. The darkness as regards my late father's passing and the heaviness which comes with that has made me something of a hermit these last few years. I trust Lord Wrexham entirely, of course." His head tilted and his gaze swept over her again, making her blush, her cheeks warming. "I think I can learn to trust you too."

"I hope you can." Rachel looked away from him, afraid that somehow, he would see the warmth in her face and realize what such a look was doing to her heart. "As I was saying, Your Grace, I spoke to my father about such matters because I had come to a decision."

The Duke offered her his arm again and they resumed their walk. "Might I ask what that decision is?"

With a deep breath, Rachel set her shoulders and, lifting her chin, told him the truth. "I have decided to accept your offer, Your Grace. I will accept your courtship."

The breath of relief which came from him made Rachel's heart jump with surprise. She had not expected him to appear so and yet he seemed to be more than a little delighted with her response.

"You cannot know of my gratitude in this, Miss Grifford. I believe I will need all the aid you can offer," he told her, his words coming quick and fast, tumbling over each other as he spoke. "You will not be aware of this as yet, but I was poisoned again only a few days ago. Thankfully, I did not eat enough to kill me but the opportunity was there for it."

Stunned, Rachel stumbled just a little but the Duke caught her, his eyes filled with a new concern.

"I am quite all right," she said quickly, looking up at him. "But you were almost poisoned? In what way? Was it the whiskey?"

The Duke shook his head. "No. A footman brought a tray of Queen's Currant Cakes to myself and Lord Wrexham and I will confess a weakness for those particular cakes. I took one and began to eat it at once, not noticing that the footman had stepped away from us both without offering Lord Wrexham something from the tray. Lord Wrexham, seeing this, thought that there might be something awry and knocked the cake from my hand... and from my mouth!"

"Good gracious!"

The Duke offered her a small smile. "I then fainted."

Rachel found herself clutching at his arm, her eyes going wide as the Duke nodded.

"But Lord Wrexham and my cousin took me to rest in the parlour and I quickly recovered. The doctor was sent for but then dismissed given how quickly I was able to recover myself. Whatever was in the cakes was not enough for me to be overcome by it given how little I had eaten."

"I see." Rachel's hand slowly uncurled from the Duke's arm, a little embarrassed at how fervently she had reacted. "That is a relief, at least."

"Yes, a very great relief!" the Duke chuckled, surprising her at the lightness in his voice. "But I must admit, I am rather concerned still that this person is so determined in their attempts to injure me."

Rachel considered this for a moment. "It must have been someone who was present last evening," she said, slowly, thinking hard. "Might I ask if there were any gentlemen present who were known both to your father and to yourself?"

"Plenty," came the heavy reply. "I could not tell you all of their names, though I did write down who I remembered once I returned home."

"That is something, at least." Rachel looked up at him again. "So, if we are to court, then the *ton* will be aware of it and will not think twice about seeing us in company together. It will give me opportunity to be watchful also and I fully intend to devote myself to that purpose at the next social gathering we enjoy."

The Duke reached across and pressed her hand as it sat on his arm, a long breath escaping him. "You are truly wonderful, Miss Grifford. I cannot imagine who it might be, I cannot even think as to who this person is and yet knowing that Lord Wrexham and you are seeking to aid me does bring me comfort. I do not feel as alone."

Rachel smiled back at him. "You are not alone," she promised, quietly. "We will discover the truth, Your Grace. I am quite certain of it."

As she spoke, a sudden thought entered her mind, making her smile fix in place as she caught her breath. It was a sudden, sharp imagining and Rachel did not know what to make of it.

"What is it?"

She shook her head, not wanting to make the Duke aware of her thoughts for they were a little too concerning and not something she dared to say aloud for fear that he would firstly, be very angry with her and secondly, throw such a thought aside.

"It is nothing of importance," she said, choosing to set that to one side for the moment. "Might I ask if you will speak to my father soon?"

"This very afternoon, if he has time to speak with me," the Duke replied, making her eyes flare in surprise. "Do you think he would be willing?"

"I think he would be more than willing," Rachel answered, her heart beating a little faster at the thought of their courtship becoming known to all of society. "So it will be told to the *ton* this evening, mayhap?"

The Duke nodded. "Yes, I think so. Would you be contented with that?"

Rachel swallowed and then nodded. "Yes, of course," she agreed, despite the nervousness running through her. "This evening, we shall tell all we know that we are courting."

Chapter Sixteen

"You certainly have caused a bit of an uproar this evening."

Andrew scowled. "It was not intentional."

Lord Wrexham chuckled. "You appear to be a little upset that your announcement about your courtship has garnered so much attention. Did you think it would not?"

"I was not prepared for the level of conversation that would flood around me because of it," Andrew admitted, his expression still rather heavy. "I did not think that this would rattle around the ballroom with such fervour."

Lord Wrexham chuckled. "Surely you must understand the surprise! You are a somewhat objectionable gentleman, who has refused to dance, refused to even *speak* to those in the *ton* and yet now, you are courting Miss Grifford! She, who is a very pretty, amiable young lady and you, who is a grumpy, unsettled, dark-natured fellow... well, you can see why there might be so much surprise!"

"I danced with Miss Grifford *and* with Miss Renfrew on some occasions," Andrew protested weakly, though he quickly saw his friend rolling his eyes and knew exactly how foolish his protestations were. "Very well, I will admit to all of that. But all the same – "

"I do not think that you should end your courtship."

Andrew blinked rapidly, confusion mounting in his heart. "I beg your pardon?"

"You ought not to end your courtship," Lord Wrexham repeated. "Yes, I know you have only just agreed to it, the *ton* has only just become aware of it but I do not think that you will *ever* find as agreeable a young lady as Miss Grifford. Do not look at her as the means to an end but rather consider her as a potential future. Do you not think that your future would be very bright indeed with her in it?"

Clearing his throat, Andrew folded his arms and looked away, finding the whole conversation very confusing indeed. "I do not think that I need to consider anything akin to that as yet. The only thing I am searching for at present is the person responsible for attempting to injure me."

Lord Wrexham sighed. "You are not listening to me. You are thinking solely about the present and not the future."

"That is because there can be no future unless I discover the truth of the present!" Andrew exclaimed. "Though I do understand what you mean about Miss Grifford. I will admit to that."

"Good. That is something at least." Lord Wrexham smiled and then looked across the room. "Are you going to step out from the shadows and face the *ton*? Or are you going to hide yourself away for the rest of the evening and leave Miss Grifford to answer all the questions?"

Andrew turned his attention back to where Miss Grifford was standing, having been observing her for some minutes. She had been surrounded by young ladies at one point and he had seen the way her eyes had widened in surprise at the sheer amount of attention she had been given. He had not gone to her, had chosen to remain where he was rather than going to join her and a swell of guilt *had* erupted over him – but he had ignored it. If she was able to control the conversation and answer the questions from every young lady present, then he would not have to join her.

"You cannot continue to hide yourself away." His friend put a hand on his shoulder for only a moment. "Do not go back to the gentleman you were at the start of the Season, I beg of you."

Andrew frowned. "What do you mean?"

"Do not go back to hiding yourself here, refusing to speak to anyone and pretending that you are not even present," Lord Wrexham stated, speaking clearly and firmly so that Andrew could not miss his meaning. "You are courting Miss Grifford now, which means that you will have to do all that you can to support her in public."

The guilt which Andrew had pushed away before began to now rise up within him again and this time, there was no way to escape it. With a long sigh, he shook his head and then looked away from his friend. "Very well."

"Be cautious still, however," Lord Wrexham warned. "Whoever is behind the attacks on you might take advantage of this moment since your attention will be on other things."

With a nod, Andrew strode forward and casting his fears aside, made his way towards Miss Grifford. He saw the moment that the young ladies took note of his arrival, for one nudged another and within a few minutes, every single eye was upon him.

"Miss Grifford." Andrew spoke a little more loudly than before so as to be heard over the crowd. "I recall that I have not signed your dance card as yet."

She smiled at him though it did not reach her eyes as she handed him her dance card. "Of course, Your Grace."

He signed it without really looking at it, though he made sure to take the waltz. It would be expected for him to take the waltz and he had to admit to himself that he had enjoyed dancing that with her.

"It is so exciting to hear that you are courting Miss Grifford," one of the ladies said, her eyes flickering with an emotion that Andrew could not quite make out. "What was it about her that caught your attention?"

"Especially when she has an older sister," said another, tilting her head so that she could study him a little more carefully. "Did Miss Bettina Grifford not come into your view at all?"

Andrew blinked, a little surprised at the question and finding himself rather embarrassed that the lady thought it was quite all right for her to speak in this way. "I – "

"It is rather improper for you to suggest that the Duke ought to court someone else, Miss Kensington," another lady said before Andrew could speak any further. "Especially when the lady herself is present!"

Realizing that the lady speaking was none other than Miss Renfrew, Andrew let out a slow breath and then offered her a small smile, which she returned.

"I chose Miss Grifford – Miss *Rachel* Grifford – because she is the one who piqued my interest," he stated, noticing how Miss Kensington frowned and Miss Grifford herself flushed. "Now, Miss Grifford, might you like to take a walk around the ballroom? Miss Renfrew, would you like to join us as chaperone?"

Miss Renfrew grinned. "I should like it very much."

Miss Grifford nodded but said nothing, coming to stand beside Andrew and then taking his arm, following along with him as they walked away together. Miss Renfrew fell into step beside her, though much to Andrew's surprise, Lord Wrexham appeared also, perhaps having listened to the entire conversation.

"I thought I might walk with you, Miss Renfrew," he said, throwing her a smile. "It may be that the Duke and Miss Grifford will have opportunity then to speak together without fear of being overheard by us!"

Miss Renfrew quickly agreed and though they walked beside them still, Andrew was now able to converse with Miss Grifford without interruption though, as he looked at her, he found himself struggling to know what to say, his thoughts beginning to whir one over the other.

"Miss Grifford," he began, stammering a little, "I – I do hope that you were not too upset by all those questioning you. If they were anything akin to that last one, then that must have been very troubling."

She glanced at him, then shook her head. "They were not too difficult to answer," she replied, her voice a little quiet so that he had to strain to hear her. "I suppose it should be expected."

"Mayhap." A sense of protectiveness rose up over him and he frowned hard, wondering at the unsettling sensation. It was not something that he had expected to feel as regarded Miss Grifford and strangely, it had only grown within him as they had commenced their courtship.

"They were very fervent with their questions," Miss Grifford continued, offering him a wry smile. "But I was able to answer them all."

"Your father was very fervent also this afternoon," Andrew told her, making her eyes alight with a sudden good humor. "Did I tell you that I did not even have to ask him to court you? He shook my hand and told me that I already had his permission to court you. I did not even need to speak a word!"

Miss Grifford laughed and as she did so, Andrew felt her relax. It was as though all the tension which she had carried with her since the barrage of questions had faded simply from being in his company.

"I do look forward to dancing with you this evening," he said, quietly. "I think it will be a very pleasant evening in that regard, at least."

"Though we must still consider who it is that is pursuing your harm," came the reply, that smile fading. "I think – "

Andrew shook his head, finding himself speaking before he even had a chance to think of what he wanted to say. "I think I should like it if we did what we could to enjoy this evening rather than worry about who is doing what behind my back. There is a great deal to think on at the moment, Miss Grifford but for this evening, might we consider only what we have told the *ton*? It is a significant enough event for us to be courting and that, perhaps, is all we ought to be considering this evening. Mayhap we might find ourselves enjoying it for a short while rather than worrying about everything else."

Her steps slowed and she turned her head to look at him a little more fully, making Andrew's stomach twist. He had not intended to say such a thing but seeing what she had endured with the questions and now aware of the worry on her face, Andrew found himself eager to settle that within her just a little.

"That would be very pleasant," she said, after a few moments, her smile sending a fresh lightness into his heart. "Thank you, Your Grace. Though you should still be careful."

"Oh, I shall be," he agreed with a half-smile. "I have decided I shall not eat a single thing this evening or, in fact, drink anything without pouring it myself. In that regard, I think I shall be quite all right."

Miss Grifford's smile grew all the brighter and with a nod, she continued walking with him again. "That sounds very sensible, Your Grace."

"Andrew."

Her head turned again sharply, blinking up at him.

"You should call me Andrew, though only when we are in private conversation," he explained, seeing the way her eyes flared. "That is, only if you should like to."

A touch of pink came into Miss Grifford's cheeks and after a moment, she nodded though the smile she offered him was a little shy. "I should like to. But you may then call me Rachel, if you wish."

"Rachel." Her name on his lips made the warmth in her cheeks grow all the more and Andrew found himself smiling back at her. They had only agreed to commence their courtship this afternoon and yet, already, he felt a strengthening of their connection.

That brought to mind a troubling thought. Lord Wrexham had already suggested that even should the truth be discovered as to who was doing this to him, he should keep his courtship with Miss Grifford maintained. But if he did so, that would lead to engagement and, subsequently, to marriage.

That was a most terrifying prospect, was it not? Or was it the most wonderful thing he had ever permitted himself to contemplate?

"Cousin."

Andrew turned, a little surprised at the sharpness of Lord Chiddick's voice. "Chiddick. Good evening."

His cousin did not smile. "I have just heard the most incredible news."

"Oh?"

Lord Chiddick lifted his chin a notch. "I have been told of a courtship."

"Ah." Andrew smiled and shrugged. "It has spread through this ballroom with the greatest speed. I did not think that there would be that much interest and yet –"

"You are courting Miss Grifford?"

Andrew stopped, a little surprised that not only had his cousin interrupted him, but also that there was a sharp anger to his tone which Andrew did not understand. He took in Lord Chiddick, noticing the way his brows hung low over his eyes, how shadows crossed his expression as he folded his arms across his chest.

"Yes," he said slowly, trying to understand Lord Chiddick's reaction. "I am. Does that trouble you in some way?"

"What troubles me is that you did not tell me of this," came the quick reply, a slight narrowing coming through Lord Chiddick's eyes. "Do you not understand? I am your *cousin* and yet you told me nothing of this! Can you imagine my embarrassment at hearing of this from Lord Henderson? Lord Henderson asked me why I was unaware of it and I could give him no answer!"

Still rather taken aback by Lord Chiddick's reaction, Andrew spread out both hands. "I did not think that you would be at all angry about such a thing. It all came about rather quickly."

"And unexpectedly," Lord Chiddick stated, his arms still tight across his chest. "I did not even know you were *thinking* of courting the lady! The last I heard, you were quite determined not to even think of such a thing. Why then have you changed your mind?"

Andrew considered this, wondering whether he ought to tell his cousin the truth about everything, only to recall Lord

Wrexham's advice. At the same time, he remembered his considerations as regarded continuing the courtship and that sealed his lips.

"I like Miss Grifford," he said, eventually. "That is all."

Lord Chiddick rolled his eyes. "That is unusual."

"Why should it be?"

"Because you have been quite determined *not* to pursue a young lady!" came the angry reply. "And now you do this?! It does not make any sense to me. I –"

"Oh."

Evidently hearing Andrew's low murmur, Lord Chiddick stopped dead and narrowed his gaze a little more. "What is it?"

"You... you care for Miss Grifford?" Andrew tilted his head, studying his cousin. "Is this the reason for your upset? I did not know that you were considering her but now that I think of it, you *were* the one who wished to call on her, to have her introduced to you and the like. I am sorry, cousin. I did not think of that for a moment."

Lord Chiddick opened his mouth and then closed it again before dropping his arms to his sides with a long and heavy sigh. He looked away and then passed one hand over his eyes.

"Forgive me, cousin. I did not mean to speak with such fierceness," he said, a good deal more quietly than before. "If I am to be truthful, I was very surprised indeed to hear that you were not only courting but courting Miss Grifford – Miss *Rachel* Grifford at that!"

A streak of anger raced up to Andrew's heart. "Miss Rachel Grifford is an exceptional young lady."

"Oh, I am well aware of that!" Lord Chiddick responded with a smile. "It is only that her sister is so... well, a good deal more prominent in society than Rachel. However, as I was saying, I was surprised to hear your news and, thereafter, felt myself embarrassed that I did not know it before anyone else. Being family, I assumed that I would have been told by you beforehand." He let out another sigh and then shook his head. "And I will admit to a fleeting interest in Miss Grifford though it is not as though I had any real intention of pursuing that."

"I see." Satisfied that he now understood his cousin's upset, Andrew reached out one hand to shake Lord Chiddick's. "Forgive me for my lack of consideration. As I am sure you are well aware, I am not exactly well known for my thoughts as regards the satisfaction of others."

Lord Chiddick offered him a wry smile but shook Andrew's hand firmly. "Forgive me for my own frustration. I ought not to have been so sharp in my words." He released Andrew's hand and then winked. "Though if you decide to end the courtship, please do tell me before anyone else – even before Miss Grifford!"

"So that you can step in instead?" Andrew asked, finding himself rather despondent at the idea rather than laughing along with his cousin.

"Yes, precisely!" Lord Chiddick grinned and then with a shrug, turned away. "I think Miss Grifford an exceptional young lady, just as you have said. Perhaps I ought to have stepped in sooner rather than wait to see if anyone else caught my attention!" He chuckled as he spoke the final few words over his shoulder. "Should I be given opportunity, I will not make that same mistake again!"

Andrew scowled and walked away in the opposite direction. His cousin had clearly had an interest in Miss Grifford but Andrew had been entirely unaware of it. Would he give up Miss Grifford, knowing that Lord Chiddick was ready to step in to take her into his arms? Or was he beginning to find himself even more protective of the lady than ever before?

Chapter Seventeen

"So you are soon to be engaged, I am sure."

Rachel's heart slammed against her ribs and she looked at Miss Renfrew with wide eyes. "Engaged? No, I certainly do not believe so. The Duke of Longford is only courting me at present and –"

"The gentleman has been absent from London for some years," her friend interrupted. "He has returned to London and in only a short while, seeks to court you! There must be something of significance in that, I am sure."

Rachel hesitated, remembering how the Duke had asked her not to tell anyone about the true reason behind their courtship and yet finding herself eager to share something with her friend. "It may not be as you think," she said, slowly. "The Duke has a reason for courting me and it is not because of interest."

Miss Renfrew frowned. "No?"

Rachel shook her head but said nothing more.

"Your father and mother must be delighted, however, "Miss Renfrew continued, as Rachel offered her a small smile. "Though I cannot imagine that your sister is delighted?"

Wincing, Rachel permitted herself a small, wry laugh. "Bettina has been throwing things for the last three days," she admitted, seeing Miss Renfrew scowl. "My courtship was announced only four days ago and in that time, though Bettina has behaved perfectly at every social occasion, she has been like a whirlwind back at home. The maids duck every time they step into the room and even our father has been unable to calm her!"

"Goodness, that does sound rather serious."

"The Duke of Longford does not know of it, however, though I am sure he will be able to guess at her response to our courtship. Though I dread to think of her dark words to me when the courtship comes to an end!"

"What?"

Too late did Rachel realize that she had spoken without thinking. Her eyes closed briefly and she stammered an explanation, but nothing made sense.

"Tell me the truth," Miss Renfrew demanded, her hand going out to grasp Rachel's as they stood in the middle of the London street, passersby going here and there. "What are you talking about? Why should your engagement come to an end?"

Rachel swallowed the lies she had been about to offer as explanation, knowing that she could not easily lie to her friend. Miss Renfrew had been nothing but generous to her and Rachel did not want to tell untruths. "I cannot tell you everything but only to state that the Duke requires my help. There is someone who is seeking to injure him and given that my status has been rather lowly in society, I thought I might be able to aid him by watching him and seeing what takes place."

Miss Renfrew's eyes rounded though she said nothing.

"I understand that this will come as a great astonishment to you," Rachel continued, slowly, "but I must beg of you to keep it all to yourself for the moment. I dare not have it shared with anyone."

"But of course, of course!" Miss Renfrew exclaimed, staring at Rachel as though she had never seen her before. "But why should he then seek to court you? I do not understand."

Quickly, Rachel explained all, seeing Miss Renfrew never blink even once as she listened to everything Rachel said. "Thus," she said, finishing, "once this person is unmasked, there will be no need for such things as our courtship. Though," she admitted, a little ruefully, "this has not worked as I thought. I believed that the courtship was simply to permit us to have conversations and the like without anyone noticing."

"Except all of the *ton* has become very excited to hear such news and everyone is talking about it," Miss Renfrew finished, shaking her head. "That is because the Duke was rather beastly and then, all of a sudden, he declares that he is courting you? Of course it would be a great surprise! Little wonder that everyone is speaking of it."

"Indeed," Rachel sighed, smiling as she slipped her arm through Miss Renfrew's and continued to walk. "Though I must beg of you again not to say a word of this to anyone. It has been of great concern to me that the Duke has avoided disaster on two occasions for they have both been entirely unexpected and come as a great shock to him."

"And because you care for him," Miss Renfrew said, practically. "You may have given me this prolonged explanation,

Rachel, but I quite believe that you will be engaged to him regardless of what happens. I only hope that he will live long enough to see that!"

Rachel closed her eyes briefly and then shook her head, choosing not to respond to her friend. In truth, she did not know what to say, for there was such a confusion within her own heart that she dared not even think of it for fear of what it would bring to her mind.

"Shall we go the bookshop?" Miss Renfrew's tone was light, as though she was pleased that Rachel had said nothing in response, perhaps aware that Rachel was struggling with her own feelings. "I think that – "

"Is that not Lord Chiddick?" Rachel stopped suddenly, looking at the gentleman as he climbed down from his carriage. "He spoke to me at the ball and congratulated me on the courtship though he did not smile a great deal. I think he is a very amiable gentleman, do you not?"

Miss Renfrew nodded. "I suppose so, though I do not know him particularly well." She tilted her head and looked sidelong at Rachel. "Did he not call on you? Mayhap that is why he did not smile so much, for perhaps he hoped to court you instead of the Duke!"

Rachel laughed and made to move forward, only to see Lord Chiddick enter into the apothecary. At the very same time, the thought which had struck her once before came back to her again – and she snatched in a breath.

"Rachel?" Miss Renfrew frowned, looking at her strangely. "Whatever is the matter? You have gone rather pale and – "

"Grace, you must do something for me." Turning to her, Rachel grasped her friend's hands, staring straight into her eyes. "Please, do not ask me for an explanation for there is not time. I will tell you all thereafter."

Miss Renfrew blinked but nodded. "Very well. What can I do?"

"Go into the apothecary and see what Lord Chiddick purchases," Rachel begged her, squeezing her hands. "Please, make yourself as discreet as possible so that he does not recognise you. If I go in, I am sure he will see my face and know it but he is not as well acquainted with you."

Miss Renfrew opened her mouth and then closed it again, a steely look coming into her eyes. "Very well," she said, as Rachel closed her eyes in relief. "Where will you be?"

"The bookshop," Rachel suggested, as her friend nodded. "I cannot be seen. Please hurry, Grace. It is of the utmost importance!"

Without another word, Miss Renfrew turned and hurried towards the apothecary. Rachel, though she longed to wait outside and watch to see what might happen, forced herself to walk towards the bookshop, aware of the trembling which had taken a hold of her frame. That thought was not something she could escape, not now that she had seen Lord Chiddick enter that particular shop. Surely it could not be as she thought, for that would mean the very worst of things, the most dreadful of circumstances but yet, it lingered in her mind nonetheless.

The bell to the bookshop tinkled as she pushed open the door. Without so much as a glance in the bookshop keeper's direction, Rachel hurried to the window and, grasping a book at random, opened it and held it in her hands but kept her gaze fixed to what was going on outside.

There was no sign of either Miss Renfrew or Lord Chiddick. Rachel's breathing grew quicker as she pressed her free hand to her stomach, aware of the tension there. *It would make sense,* she thought to herself, her worries rising steadily as she continued to gaze outside, waiting for someone to appear. *It could be that Lord Chiddick is the one attempting to harm the Duke, though quite what his purpose could be for that, I do not know.*

She closed her eyes for a moment and took in a deep breath, trying to steady herself. Swallowing her fears, she steadied herself and opened her eyes again, only to see Lord Chiddick striding back towards his carriage. Of Miss Renfrew, there was no sign.

Setting the book back down, Rachel made to hurry out again, though she waited for Lord Chiddick to climb back into his carriage and then drive away again so that he would not see her emerging from the bookshop. It took her only a few moments to make her way from the bookshop to the apothecary and, stepping inside, quickly found Miss Renfrew.

"Well?" She gripped Miss Renfrew's hand, seeing her friend's eyebrows furrowing. "Did you see what it was that he bought?"

"A few things," Miss Renfrew replied, keeping her voice quiet as she glanced over her shoulder to where the apothecary himself was standing at the counter. "Laudanum, a scent of some sort and I did overhear him asking for something to deter rats."

"Deter rats?" Rachel repeated, a knot forming in her stomach. "That is something that one's servants would do usually, is it not?"

"Yes, I suppose it is." Miss Renfrew frowned, pressing Rachel's hand. "You have not explained anything to me as yet. Why should such a thing trouble you? Why should Lord Chiddick's presence be so distressing?"

"Because," Rachel whispered as the door opened to admit another gentleman and lady, "I fear that the person responsible for injuring the Duke of Longford might very well be his cousin."

It took Miss Renfrew a few moments to respond. She simply gazed back into Rachel's face, taking in what had been said and then, much to Rachel's relief, shook her head and blew out a slow breath. "Goodness. That is rather worrying."

"I do not understand what his motivations might be but all the same, given what I know of the Duke of Longford and his situation, I am concerned that there is some particular reason for his intentions." Rachel released her friend's hand. "I must go and speak to him at once."

"To the Duke?"

Rachel nodded. "Do you think we might return home? Since we came in your carriage, I can always hail a hackney if you would prefer but – "

"No, let us go at once. I will come with you, if you wish? It will keep everyone contented as regards propriety."

Relief coursed into every part of Rachel's veins. "Thank you, my friend. Hurry. The sooner I can get to him, the happier I shall be."

***

"Your Grace?"

Rachel hurried into the room, her heart beating furiously as she saw him rise to his feet, a smile on his face. The butler had only just announced them to the Duke of Longford but Rachel had no time to wait. "Thank goodness you are home. There is something I must speak to you about at once. I – "

"Good afternoon, Lord Chiddick."

Rachel blinked in surprise, hearing Miss Renfrew's loud voice from behind her. She turned, only to see Lord Chiddick bowing towards Miss Renfrew. Her whole body went cold as she smiled, then looked back at the Duke who was looking at her with concern in his eyes.

"Good afternoon, Miss Grifford." Lord Chiddick bowed to her and then smiled warmly. "Forgive me. I can take my leave if there is something so urgent that you must speak to His Grace without pause?"

"Oh, no, please," Rachel found herself saying, her smile fixed as she sat down in a chair, Miss Renfrew doing the same. "It is not at all serious."

"No?" Lord Chiddick kept smiling as he sat down. "It certainly sounded serious."

Rachel let out a broken laugh, looking to Miss Renfrew in the hope that she would be able to help her. "It may have sounded so but it is not truly serious in any way."

"Unless you are concerned about the snubbing of the Duke to a dinner party!" Miss Renfrew exclaimed, laughing with a shake of her head. "We spoke to a particular friend who informed us that she has heard that a prominent dinner party is soon to take place but even though Miss Grifford's family will be invited, His Grace will be absent from the invited guests!"

Rachel nodded fervently, seeing the Duke's smile fixing to his face and wondering if he knew that this was all a pretense or if he was truly concerned about this dinner party. "I thought to tell you, Your Grace but now that Miss Renfrew says it in that way, I realise that there is nothing of concern. Not really."

"It is still a little troubling, yes," Lord Chiddick replied before the Duke could say anything. "Why should anyone wish to ignore you, cousin?" A tiny smile edged up one side of his mouth. "Could it be because your demeanour is still rather dark? Even though you have begun courting Miss Grifford, there are clearly those who have not yet warmed to you!" He began to chuckle and Rachel forced herself to smile back at him, even though her stomach was twisting furiously, her worries almost insurmountable. They had not been far behind Lord Chiddick but had there still been enough opportunity for him to do *something* to him, had there not? What if he had already been poisoned?

"Shall I send for tea?" The Duke lifted one eyebrow just a little as Rachel found herself nodding. "You will stay for a little while?"

"Yes, if that suits Miss Renfrew?" Looking over her shoulder, Rachel saw her friend nodding and after that, let her eyes turn to Lord Chiddick who, much to Rachel's distress, was also nodding with a smile on his face. Was there going to be a chance for her to tell the Duke of Longford what she suspected? Or was Lord Chiddick going to stand in her way?

Chapter Eighteen

There is something wrong.

Andrew watched Miss Renfrew and then turned his attention to Miss Grifford, noticing how her lip caught between her teeth for just a moment as she glanced to Lord Chiddick and then looked away again. Though he wanted to ask her what the trouble was, recalling how she had rushed into the room and spoken to him with such fervor, it was clear to him that there was something that she wanted to speak of and he certainly did not believe that it had anything to do with a dinner party. He did not know Miss Grifford extremely well as yet but what he did know of her told him that she was troubled. The way she had laughed and smiled about the dinner party had been without any true mirth, without any genuine spark of laughter in her eyes and he had felt his stomach drop.

Something had happened. Something that she wanted to tell him, something that she had to tell him without delay and yet, at the present moment, she could not.

It is because Chiddick is here.

Andrew frowned and rubbed one hand over his chin. This was a little concerning. Lord Chiddick was his cousin and yet Miss Grifford did not feel able to speak in front of him.

Then again, he reminded himself, as Miss Renfrew and Lord Chiddick laughed about some matter or other, *I did beg her not to speak of my situation and I did inform her that only Lord Wrexham was aware of it. Perhaps that is why she does not want to tell me anything in front of Lord Chiddick.*

"It is getting a little late and my mother will require me home very soon." Miss Renfrew sighed and rose to her feet, looking to Miss Grifford who, with a nod, shot Andrew a look and then turned her head away. "I am sorry to have to take our leave when we have been enjoying such prolonged conversations."

"Enjoyable conversations also," Lord Chiddick said, smiling as he got to his feet. "Will you be attending Lord Huddersfield's ball this evening?"

Andrew looked to Miss Grifford as she nodded but noticed how she looked up to him again.

His heart slammed hard against his ribs. She needed him. She needed to speak with him and yet could not. What was he going to do?

"If you are going to be a little tardy, might I suggest that I bring my carriage around and take you home, Miss Grifford?" he asked, seeing her eyes flare. "That way, Miss Renfrew would be able to return home without diverting."

"I should like that very much. I have my maid and –"

"You need not trouble yourself, cousin!" Lord Chiddick walked across the room and put one hand onto his shoulder. "I have my carriage. Rather than having the difficulty of having your carriage called around, it would be much easier if I took the lady, would it not?"

Andrew cleared his throat and threw his cousin what he hoped appeared to be a playful wink. "It would be easier, I am sure but I would much prefer to go to the difficulty of calling the carriage and taking Miss Grifford back myself."

Lord Chiddick chuckled and shrugged. "Very well, if you are sure. It would be no trouble."

Andrew glanced to Miss Grifford and noticed the slight paleness to her cheeks and the way her eyes had flared. "I think not, cousin, though I thank you again for your kind and most generous offer. Miss Grifford? Might I walk you to the door where we will await the carriage? It will not take more than a few minutes."

"But of course." With what looked like a relieved smile, Miss Grifford took his arm but her fingers grasped it so tightly, it was clear just how tense she now felt. Andrew smiled briefly and walked to the door with her, with Miss Renfrew and Lord Chiddick following thereafter – though it was Miss Renfrew who continued a conversation with Lord Chiddick, leaving Andrew to murmur quietly to Miss Grifford.

"Are you quite all right?"

She glanced at him. "I need to speak with you. It is of the greatest urgency."

"In the carriage, then," he murmured, as she nodded. "It will not be long now." They managed to keep up an amiable conversation while both Lord Chiddick and Miss Renfrew waited with them for the carriage to arrive but with every second that passed, Andrew could feel the tension beginning to tighten his stomach and rush through his frame. What was it that she wanted to tell him?

"Ah, here we are." With a smile of relief, Andrew stepped forward and took Miss Grifford's hand, ready to help her up to the carriage. "Good afternoon, Lord Chiddick, Miss Renfrew. We will see you both again this evening."

With a nod, Lord Chiddick smiled and turned away and, with relief, Andrew climbed into the carriage behind Miss Grifford.

"It is your cousin!"

The moment he sat down, Miss Grifford leaned forward and grasped one of his hands, leaving Andrew to rap on the roof so that the carriage trundled forward. He blinked, seeing the wide-eyed look she offered him, the way the color drained from her face as though she was now afraid of what his response would be.

"I am afraid I do not understand, Miss Grifford," Andrew said softly, turning his hand so that he could thread his fingers through hers. "Explain to me what you mean and have no fear in speaking honestly. I will not be in the least bit upset or angry with anything you have to tell me."

Miss Grifford closed her eyes and nodded, letting out a long, slow breath before she began again. "That is a relief to hear from you, Andrew, for what I have to say is significant." Opening her eyes again, she looked back at him steadily. "I have reason to believe that it is your cousin who is behind all of this."

"Chiddick?" Still confused, Andrew's eyebrows knotted. "I do not understand."

"My dear Andrew, I may be entirely mistaken but permit me to explain myself clearly," Miss Grifford began, her voice wobbling a little. "This afternoon, Miss Renfrew and I were out walking through town and I saw your cousin step out of his carriage. I was going to speak with him, I was going to call to him simply to greet him when I saw him step into the apothecary."

"That is not very surprising," Andrew said, speaking slowly as he fought to understand. "Any number of gentlemen and ladies might go to the apothecary."

"But would they go to purchase something that a servant would usually be sent for?"

Andrew sat back in his seat and released Miss Grifford's hand, a fear beginning to writhe in his stomach like a snake. "What happened?"

Miss Grifford clasped her hands together though her eyes still fixed to his. "I sent Miss Renfrew into the apothecary for fear that I would be recognised – though he is acquainted with Miss Renfrew but does not know her particularly well. I hid in the bookshop, waited until he departed and then found Miss Renfrew again, eager to know what it was that he had purchased."

"And what was it?"

Miss Grifford swallowed. "Laudanum, a scent of some kind and from what Miss Renfrew overheard, a poison for rats."

"Which is not something that any gentleman would purchase," Andrew said slowly, seeing what she meant. "A servant would be left to deal with rats. Why would a gentleman purchase such a thing?"

Miss Grifford nodded, her lip caught between her teeth for a moment before she took in another breath, blew it out and then continued. "I must ask you something, Andrew. Would there be any reason that your cousin would seek to not only harm you but also harm your father?"

Andrew sucked in a breath, shock rattling through him. He had never once considered his cousin, had never once imagined that there would be any sort of motivation for Lord Chiddick to harm not only Andrew's father but Andrew himself – but now that Miss Grifford presented it to him, he knew exactly why Lord Chiddick might have been doing such a thing.

"I do."

Miss Grifford gasped, her eyes rounding as though she had hoped that what she had told him would prove to be some sort of mistake, a mix-up which would not make Lord Chiddick have any sort of guilt whatsoever.

"He is the heir," Andrew said, quietly, passing one hand over his eyes as his shoulders rounded, a weight settling upon his heart. "I have no brother to speak of, no uncles or the like. The only person who would take on my title, should I pass away from this life, would be my cousin."

Miss Grifford closed her eyes tightly and Andrew reached out, grasping her hand and feeling how cold it was in his own.

"You have found out the truth," he told her, hating that his heart was pounding so furiously, it felt as though he had been running for a long distance. "I think this must be it. This must be exactly what it is. *Chiddick* is the one who has been attempting to injure me." Another thought came to him and sweat broke out across his forehead, a heavy breath escaping him. "He knows my penchant for Queen Currant Cakes. That would make sense now, would it not?"

"Oh, Andrew."

The way she spoke his name, the sympathy and the sweetness which rushed through her voice made his heart lift, despite the heaviness which grasped it and tried to drag it down.

"You are quite wonderful, Miss Grifford," he told her, looking back into her face and pushing his fingers through hers once more, feeling the urge to hold onto her, not to release her from his grip. "I will not pretend that I am not sorrowful about this. I am not going to lie and say that I am nothing but relieved and now I shall be very contented for I am deeply troubled and rather upset. But yet, my heart is filled with a gratitude for you and what you have not only learned but the courage you have in coming to tell me – knowing that it is my cousin of whom you speak."

Her eyes softened, her shoulders dropping in evident relief. "You can see now why I came thundering into your house as I did. I was so afraid that something would happen to you before I could reach you and when I saw Lord Chiddick there, my fear grew all the more."

"I quite understand," Andrew said, offering her a small smile. "I must think about what I am to do now. I do not know how I am to protect myself – and protect you – from my cousin while, at the same time, finding a way to reveal his actions to not only myself but to society at large. It is the only way I can stop him." Letting out a slow hiss, he shook his head and looked out of the window in the hope that some sort of inspiration might come to him. "Confronting him face to face will do nothing."

"Because he can do just as he pleases regardless of your confrontation," Miss Grifford murmured, understanding immediately. "It must be a public confession of some sort. He must admit to his guilt so that the *ton* will know of it and, thereafter, he will be disgraced and then rejected from society."

"It is either that or I call him out," Andrew replied, grimly, seeing her eyes flare with a sudden fear. "Though I do not want to do such a thing as that. I would not have bloodshed."

"I should not want to lose you."

The softness of her voice, the sweetness of her words and the gentle way she pressed his hand made Andrew's heart leap up and then swell with a great and wondrous delight – a delight which warmed right through him. He knew then that he could not separate himself from this lady. Yes, it seemed as though they had found the culprit, yes, there was still a great deal for him to do as regards Lord Chiddick and yes, his intention had always been to end their courtship at the time such a thing had been made clear but, as he looked into her eyes, Andrew knew that he could not. This was not something he wanted any longer. To be apart from the lady was not something he desired and though he found himself rather afraid of what was within his heart, though he found himself troubled by all that he felt, he did not shy away from it nor shrink back.

"You will not lose me," he said fervently, leaning forward so that he might look a little more deeply into her eyes. "No matter what happens, I assure you that you will not lose me."

She smiled at him then, her eyes glistening just a little as he held her gaze steady.

And then the carriage came to a stop.

"Will I still see you this evening?" she asked, as he nodded. "You will still attend the ball?"

"Yes. I shall."

"But you will take great care around Lord Chiddick, will you not?" Miss Grifford's eyes were still concerned, holding onto his. "You must be all the more cautious. I am a little concerned that he might now suspect that I have discovered the truth."

Andrew considered this and then nodded. "You fear that he might not believe the excuses Miss Renfrew and you made? To my ears they did sound believable."

Miss Grifford paused and then shrugged her shoulders. "It may be that there is nothing to fear but all the same, I find myself concerned," she said, honestly. "He might have seen Miss Renfrew in the apothecary. He might have recognised her and then for us to both burst into your drawing room could make him suspicious."

Understanding her meaning, Andrew nodded again. "Then I shall be all the more cautious," he promised, as she finally released his hand. "All will be well this evening, though mayhap Lord Wrexham and yourself might come to speak with me? I can trust him and it would be helpful to get his opinion on whatever it is I plan to do next."

"But of course." She smiled and made to take her leave, only for Andrew to reach out and catch her hand again. Desire flooded him and he lifted her hand to his lips, pressing a kiss to it so that he might show just a little of his care, consideration and affection for the lady – even though, in his heart and mind, he was still doing all he could to understand all that he felt. "Thank you, Rachel," he said softly, lifting his head just a little to look into her eyes. "Thank you for everything you have done, for your boldness, your courage and your consideration. I value it all. I value *you* more than I can say and I look forward to soon being in your company again."

Just as he finished speaking, a face suddenly appeared at the carriage door. Andrew released Miss Grifford's hand and turned his head, about to speak sharply to whichever footman had decided to interrupt them, only to come face to face with Lord Carmichael. The man's eyes rounded, taking in the scene and suddenly, Andrew found himself a little tongue tied.

"Father." Miss Grifford's voice sounded a little hoarse. "The Duke was bringing me home after an errand took a little longer than – "

"Your Grace?" Lord Carmichael looked at Andrew with a lifted eyebrow, his expression inscrutable. Andrew knew exactly what the gentleman meant for here he was, sitting with Miss Grifford in a carriage and with her hand at his lips. His heart slammed into his chest, his stomach twisting this way and that as he looked back at Miss Grifford, aware of what was required. Either he would make a profuse apology and promise that such a thing would never happen again or he would do what Lord Carmichael clearly expected, in order to maintain property.

Do not! his heart screamed as he cleared his throat, his mind whirring between one decision and the next. *You always said you would not, that you did not want to marry. Can you really be considering doing that now?*

"Yes, Lord Carmichael," he found himself saying, his lips feeling a little thick. "Forgive me, you have come upon me at just the wrong moment." With a forced smile, he looked back to Miss Grifford, seeing the way her eyes had rounded, two spots of color in either cheek. "Miss Grifford, what I was going to say was this: I think you the most remarkable creature and I have thought that all the more so with every day we have spent time together. Therefore, Miss Grifford, I wonder if you might considering accepting my hand in marriage."

Chapter Nineteen

Rachel was so shocked, she could not move. She stared back at the Duke of Longford, hearing nothing but a loud buzzing in her ears and aware of how fast her heart was pounding.

"Did you hear the Duke, Rachel?"

Her father's voice sounded like it was coming from very far away but even still, Rachel could not look at him. Instead, she saw only the Duke of Longford, taking in his expression, seeing the slight lift to his eyebrow and the swirl in his eyes. Was he being entirely serious? Or was this something that he now felt obliged to say given that they had been found in such a position in the carriage?

The Duke squeezed her hand and then looked to Lord Carmichael again. "I must apologise for not going about this the right way," he said, giving Rachel a few more moments to catch her breath, to come back to the present and think through what she was to answer. "I should have spoken with you first, Lord Carmichael. I should have come to request your permission and in truth, I was not entirely certain that I was to do such a thing today. But now that I am in company with your daughter, now that I am speaking with her and once more enjoying her company, I find myself overwhelmed with emotion. I pray for your forgiveness in that regard, Lord Carmichael."

"You have it!"

Rachel's eyes went to her father, seeing his broad smile and the light in his eyes. Clearly he was more than delighted with this present situation, thrilled with the way that the Duke had singled her out and was now hopeful of a match between them – but she did not feel the same way. Her heart was uncertain, aware of all that she felt for the Duke of Longford and how fearful she was of falling quite in love with him without such feelings being returned.

But what could she do? Could she really refuse him? Could she sit here, look back into his face and, in front of her father, chose to reject him? That would not be wise for then all of the *ton* would hear what she had said, would wonder at it and, no doubt, she would never be made such an offer again. To reject the Duke of Longford was surely to be made a spinster for who from the *ton* would attempt to seek her out thereafter? If she was not willing to accept a Duke, then the *ton* would think her unwilling to accept any gentleman, including those with a lesser title and she could not permit that to happen.

There is only one choice, she told herself firmly, her heart still racing with both fear and anticipation. *I must say yes.*

"Rachel?" Her father lifted an eyebrow gently, that smile hovering around his lips. "Have you an answer for the Duke?"

It was clear by the gentle yet happy tone of his voice that he was expecting her to agree, to accept and, with a nod, Rachel looked back to the Duke of Longford, painfully aware that this was the moment that everything was about to change for her.

"Yes, Your Grace," she said, only just then realizing how badly her voice was shaking. "Yes, I shall accept the offer of your hand in marriage."

The Duke smiled though there was no exuberance there. Instead, he simply lifted her hand to his lips and pressed another kiss to the back of it, leaving her breathless. "How wonderful," he murmured, as her father clapped his hands together, a broad grin settling on his face. "I am utterly delighted."

Rachel swallowed and tried to speak but her father interjected before she had a chance.

"We shall have to throw an engagement ball to celebrate!" he exclaimed, as the Duke nodded, smiled and then released Rachel's hand. "What say you, Your Grace?"

"I would be more than willing for that to take place," the Duke replied, as Rachel finally made her way from the carriage, her heart pulled between delight and uncertainty. "Though let us keep this engagement to ourselves for the moment, if we might, Lord Carmichael? I should not like to announce it at another gentleman's ball for that would be most improper and I fear that I should make a bit of an upset in that regard."

Lord Carmichael nodded as Rachel caught the Duke's eye, seeing him smile gently and realizing that he had said such a thing in order to give her opportunity to come to an understanding about all of this. She smiled back at him, one hand pressing lightly to her stomach so as to relieve the tension crawling through it.

"I quite understand. But do let us know when you intend to make the announcement," Lord Carmichael said, stepping back and putting one hand out to take Rachel's before setting it on his arm. "We shall keep it to the family only for the moment."

"I thank you."

Without another word – though he did give her a nod – the Duke took his leave and Rachel watched the carriage roll away.

"How absolutely wonderful!" With a hurried gait, her father turned and led Rachel up the steps towards the house, a broad grin settling on his face. "We shall have to tell everyone!"

"No, Father," Rachel said faintly, wishing that she might seat herself somewhere in utter silence so as to take in all that had just taken place. "Only Mother and Bettina for the moment and we must beg them both not to tell anyone else about all of this. You did give the Duke your word and –"

"Yes, yes." Her father waved his hand in a rather flippant manner. "We shall be cautious but it will be difficult to keep it between us all for even a short amount of time! We must hope that the Duke will make the announcement very soon."

Rachel made to say more, only for her father to start calling her mother's name as they entered the house. Lady Carmichael came out of the drawing room in a flurry, her eyes wide and staring as she took in Rachel on the arm of her father.

"Whatever has happened?"

Rachel swallowed hard as her father looked to her expectantly, seeing how Bettina had just now stepped out of the drawing room and was wandering slowly up towards them all.

She did not look in the least bit pleased.

"The Duke of Longford has asked to marry me," she said, hoarsely, as Lady Carmichael's eyes flared. "It was unexpected and came as a great surprise but –"

"Tell me that you accepted him?" Lady Carmichael screeched, grasping Rachel's hand and pressing it, hard. "Pray tell me that you accepted him?"

"Of course she did!" Lord Carmichael exclaimed, as though his wife was being more than ridiculous. "No-one could refuse a Duke!"

Rachel managed a faint smile but then felt her knees trembling just a little. She was overwhelmed, completely overwhelmed and yet her father and mother seemed quite determined to keep her here with them, to hold her fast as they heaped on questions and exclamations while all she wanted to do was to sit quietly and close her eyes so she might take everything in.

"You are engaged to the Duke of Longford?"

Bettina's loud voice echoed through the hallway and both Lord and Lady Carmichael stopped their exclamations at once, turning to look at their elder daughter.

"*You* are engaged to the Duke of Longford?" Bettina said again, her eyes narrowing. "You?"

"Yes." Rachel swallowed her worry and lifted her chin, looking straight back at Bettina as her sister advanced ever closer. "The announcement is to be made very soon, however, so we are not to speak of it this evening."

Bettina closed her eyes so tightly, small lines drew themselves around her eyes. Her breathing was coming in quick, sharp gasps and her hands curled into tight fists as her face slowly grew dark red with evident anger.

"You ought to congratulate your sister," Lady Carmichael said, as Bettina stayed precisely where she was, her whole body trembling visibly. "She is to be a Duchess! Can you imagine that?" Lady Carmichael's voice grew a little louder with excitement. "She is to be a *Duchess!*"

"It ought to have been me!"

Everyone turned as one towards Bettina, who put out one shaking hand and pointed at Rachel.

"You have stolen my chance! You have stolen *my* opportunity to become what I ought to have been! I should be the one with the Duke by my side! I ought to be the one who is engaged to someone so high up in society! Instead, I am given nothing."

"This is not a comparison," Lady Carmichael stated, firmly. "Come now, Bettina, you are being ridiculous. Instead of complaining, you ought to be thrilled with the news that your sister will be so exalted. This is a wonderful day!"

"I shall not celebrate it," Bettina stated, angrily. "I will say nothing and do nothing that will show any sort of happiness or joy for this engagement. Rachel has been given precedence over me, you have *both* shown her greater consideration and I –"

"We have done no such thing, Bettina. How dare you speak to me in such a fashion?"

Lord Carmichael's voice boomed around the hallway with a tone which Rachel had never heard before. It filled the space with authority, with frustration and with a hard, furious anger held within it which even Rachel herself shrank back from. The high color in Bettina's face quickly faded and she looked back at her father with eyes which now filled with tears.

"Do not be too harsh on her, my dear," Lady Carmichael began. "She has only just discovered that –"

"I have witnessed your behaviour this Season and found myself weary with it," Lord Carmichael continued, taking a step closer to Bettina and away from Rachel. "Your mother has endured a great deal, as has your sister and I, I confess, have been so apathetic to it, I have not permitted myself to take any great interest in it. Now, however, I see that I ought to have done something more. I should have stepped in long before now and told you that this behaviour is not going to be permitted to continue. It is an utter disgrace, Bettina, for you to behave in this fashion! It is not at all suitable for you to refuse to accept your sister's engagement with any sort of grace and instead, to complain about yourself and your own lack of attachment. Has it ever occurred to you, Bettina, that the reason *you* have not found a suitable attachment is because of your attitude? Because of your character and your poor behaviour? No gentleman wants a bride who thinks only of herself, who complains continually and demands what others have without showing any sort of grace!"

Bettina put one hand over her mouth, her eyes glassy and despite Lady Carmichael's protests, Lord Carmichael continued on regardless.

"You are not to say another word against Rachel's engagement. Wherever we go, you are to express delight and happiness for this wonderful event. And if I should hear that you have expressed *anything* akin to the opposite of that, then I shall make immediate arrangements to return you to our estate and end our Season at that very moment. Do you understand me?"

Rachel blinked in surprise at her father's harsh words, rather astonished that he had said anything to her sister and in those harsh tones. For the last few weeks, he had said nothing and had done nothing to make things at all better between them. In fact, he had seemed to stay perfectly silent, choosing to absent himself rather than help in any way and with anything. But now that she was engaged, now that she was to be a Duchess, her father had decided that enough was enough and Bettina, as well as Rachel, was entirely shocked by it.

"Do you understand me, Bettina?"

Bettina dropped her head into her hands and began to sob and Rachel, believing this was the end of the matter, began to move away. Lord Carmichael, however, gestured for her to stay and, albeit a little unwillingly, Rachel stayed exactly where she was.

"You may cry for as long as you wish but we will stay here until I hear you tell me that you understand," Lord Carmichael stated, his voice low and hard with determination. "Bettina, do you understand everything that I have told you?"

With a sudden, strange swiftness – a swiftness which told Rachel that Bettina had not been truly upset – Bettina lifted her head, dropped her hand and with a glower, nodded.

"Speak aloud," came the command and with a heavy sigh, Bettina flung out one hand towards Rachel.

"I understand," she stated, her brow now heavily furrowed. "I will show delight towards Rachel and her engagement."

"And you will not say a word about your displeasure," Lord Carmichael continued, as Bettina nodded sullenly. "Do not think that I will show you any sort of favour, Bettina. I speak quite truthfully. If I hear a single word, a single whisper, then I will make arrangements to have you taken back to the estate at once – and I will think twice before I take you back to London again."

Rachel watched as Bettina swallowed hard and this time, when her eyes filled with tears, Rachel believed them to be entirely genuine.

"Now, Rachel," her father said, turning to her with a smile which was quite at odds with all that he had just said. "Let us go to the drawing room with your mother and discuss all that has just taken place and the arrangements which now need to be made – including the ball!" The frown returned as he looked again to Bettina. "You, Bettina, will spend some time in reflection and contemplation alone. We will see you for dinner but not before."

Rachel opened her mouth to say something but was quickly led away by her father and mother, though she turned her head to look at Bettina as they made their way past. The sullen expression on her sister's face, the scowl which curled one side of her lip and the darkness in her features told Rachel that all was not well. She had no doubt that her father's threats had been quite genuine but whether Bettina did as he had demanded or not, that was all still to be seen.

***

"I have something I must tell you."

Miss Renfrew laughed and caught Rachel's hand. "Good evening to you also, my dear friend! You look… " Her smile faded. "Rather pale. Is everything quite all right?"

"I am engaged." The words began to tumble out of her mouth as she saw shock ripple across Miss Renfrew's expression. "The Duke and I were in conversation in the carriage as it arrived at my father's house. He caught my hand, lifted it to his lips and pressed a kiss to it just as my father opened the door and saw us in such a position. I did not know what was going to happen – I thought, mayhap, that the Duke would beg my father's pardon but instead, he proposed!"

Miss Renfrew caught her breath, her eyes flaring wide as though, for the very first time, she had realized exactly what it was that Rachel had been saying.

"I had no other choice but to accept… but this was never meant to happen, Grace! What am I to do? I do not think I can become a Duchess!"

Miss Renfrew pressed Rachel's hand, her smile spreading wide across her face. "This is wonderful! Of course you can be a Duchess! Whatever are you worrying about?" The more she looked into Rachel's face, the more she seemingly began to realize what was happening within Rachel's heart and with a slight widening to her eyes, she squeezed Rachel's hand tightly again. "You are in love with him?"

"In love?" Rachel shook her head, her throat constricting. "No, I cannot be in love with him but there is… there is certainly something within my heart, certainly."

"But why should that concern you?" Miss Renfrew asked, quietly, her eyes searching Rachel's. "It is quite all right for you to feel something for the gentleman. That is a good thing, is it not?"

"Not if it is not returned. I shall be broken-hearted but yet married to the Duke of Longford! He only proposed because my father found us in such a position…" she trailed off, suddenly remembering what Lord Wrexham had said. "Though mayhap I can hope that he does not entirely dislike me."

"Dislike you?" Miss Renfrew laughed and shook her head. "My dear friend, I am sure that the Duke of Longford cares for you. I have seen how he looks at you, how he considers you and how appreciative and grateful he is for you. There must be a genuine consideration there, I am sure of it. And now that this issue with Lord Chiddick is –"

"Hush, please!" Interrupting her friend, Rachel looked all around, afraid that Lord Chiddick was nearby and might overhear them. "That is not yet dealt with."

"But you told the Duke of it and he accepts it? He believes it?"

Rachel nodded. "He does. Lord Chiddick might well be the one responsible for causing the accident which took away the life of the Duke's father. The Duke told me that Lord Chiddick is the heir."

"To the Dukedom?"

Rachel nodded, seeing how her friend bit her lip. "The Duke, Lord Wrexham and I – and you also, if you wish – are to speak this evening about what we are to do next. Our engagement has also not been told to anyone else as yet. The Duke wants to throw an engagement ball and we shall announce it then." Her lips curved in a soft smile. "In truth, I believe that he saw just how overcome with surprise I was and wanted to make sure that I had some time to consider it all."

"Which is yet another way of showing you just how much he cares for you, albeit without saying a word," Miss Renfrew smiled, though her eyes flickered with concern. "Yes, I should like to be a part of that discussion if I can. Anything I can to do to be of assistance, I shall do it."

"And be near Lord Wrexham," Rachel added, seeing her friend's cheeks immediately flush. "Thank you, my friend."

"You must be careful, however," Miss Renfrew added, coming to stand a little closer to her, her voice lowering. "If Lord Chiddick discovers you are engaged to the Duke, then does that not pose another problem?"

"Problem?" Rachel repeated, as her friend nodded. "In what way?"

"You are to marry the Duke. You will be his Duchess and, as such, the one to provide the heir," Miss Renfrew said, quietly. "Might you not be putting yourself in danger also?"

Rachel considered this, nodding slowly as she looked into her friend's eyes. "You might well be right," she said, softly, her eyes rounding. "Lord Chiddick wishes to take the dukedom. But if I marry and produce the heir, as you have said, then that prevents him."

"So Lord Chiddick will have to bring an end not only to the Duke's life but also to yours," Miss Renfrew said, quietly. "Be careful, Rachel. This could be a good deal more dangerous than you think."

Chapter Twenty

"What?"

Andrew nodded. "It is just as I have said and it is all because of Miss Grifford that I have learned the truth."

Lord Wrexham went rather pale, rubbing one hand over his face. "You mean to say that your cousin is the one who caused your father's accident and has, subsequently, been attempting to poison you?"

Andrew nodded. "Yes, I believe so. He is the heir to the Dukedom since I have no brother behind me and thus, it would make sense for him to be behind this all. I confess that I am still rather stunned by it all but who else can be responsible? The Queens Currant Cakes, for example, are my favourite as I have said, but it would only be my cousin who would be aware of such a thing."

"Good gracious."

"And now I must know what I am to do," Andrew continued, seeing his friend's eyebrows lift. "How can I force his hand? How can I force him to reveal to me the truth about all of this? I must do it in a way where he is unaware but yet open enough to explain all so that *he* is disgraced and I am protected."

"You could call him out."

Andrew shook his head. "I do not want to kill him."

"Even though he has attempted to kill you?"

Considering this, Andrew still found himself against such an idea and shook his head. "No. My cousin has done a great wickedness, yes, but I do not want to act in the same way. Besides which, in calling him out and demanding a duel, do I not offer myself up to him on a silver platter?"

Lord Wrexham grimaced. "You mean to say that he could still take advantage of the situation? He could send someone to shoot you even as you are preparing for the duel."

"Leaving him as the next Duke of Longford," Andrew finished, seeing the frown on his friend's face. "So you see, it is a rather difficult situation."

Nodding, Lord Wrexham continued to consider this in silence, leaving Andrew to study him, hoping that his friend would offer something of an answer.

"Your Grace, good evening."

He turned, his heart leaping in his chest, heat spreading out across his frame and a broad smile on his face as he took in his betrothed. "Miss Grifford. You look utterly beautiful this evening." He reached for her hand and bowed over it, meaning every word. "My breath is quite gone from me."

She smiled back at him, though there was a slight flicker in her eyes which he understood. There was still a great deal of concern.

"And Miss Renfrew, good evening," Andrew continued, smiling at the lady. "I presume that Miss Grifford has explained all to you?"

"I am aware of all the recent developments, yes," came the reply, her eyes twinkling as a bright smile spread across her face. "Though I am concerned about one of them, certainly."

"Have you decided anything? Has anything been suggested to you?"

Andrew shook his head. "Only that we wish to avoid a duel at all costs."

"Quite," came the reply. "Though you must discover Lord Chiddick in public, must you not?"

A footman drew near and offered them all a brandy but Andrew declined quickly, as did the rest of them.

Miss Grifford grasped his arm. "That is it!"

He looked back at her, a little confused. "What do you mean?"

"The footman!" she exclaimed, "do you not recall? On both occasions, a footman has been used."

Andrew blinked quickly, realizing what she was saying. "The footman was instructed to bring me the poisoned whiskey and again, the cakes."

"So Lord Chiddick must be paying someone a great deal in order to have them do such a thing as that. Can we not use someone in that way? Can we not hope that he will do the very same thing at, say, our engagement ball?"

Sudden fear ripped across Andrew's chest. "You mean to suggest that we inform him of our engagement?"

Miss Grifford hesitated, then nodded. "I think we must."

"But that puts you in danger also," Miss Renfrew protested, though a steely glint came into Miss Grifford's eyes. "You have to then consider that, surely?"

"It does not matter. I am only a threat to Lord Chiddick if I marry the Duke. Before that happens, it is only the Duke of Longford himself who is in danger. Therefore, if you would arrange for the footmen that evening to be utterly loyal to you, Andrew, if you would inform them of a great reward, then if Lord Chiddick approaches one, it must be hoped that the footman would then come to you, tell you of it and you could then make a great spectacle of him."

A brief silence filled the room. "Though you would only have the word of the footman," Miss Renfrew said, slowly. "Would that be enough?"

"Leave that with me," Lord Wrexham said, grimly. "I remember the one who served the Queens Currant Cakes. I remember him well enough to find him, certainly. I can have him ready on the night of the engagement ball to declare what was being done."

"Do you think he will tell you the truth?" Andrew asked, still finding himself rather unsettled by the idea. "He would not have an incentive, surely."

Lord Wrexham's lip curled. "I will tell him that he has no other choice. I will tell him that we know it was Lord Chiddick and that anything Lord Chiddick promised him or gave him will either be doubled… or will be taken from him by way of his employment. I agree that we would not have been able to do such a thing had we not known it was Lord Chiddick but now that we do, there is nothing to prevent this from working."

Andrew turned to Miss Grifford, seeing her nodding, though he found himself a little less inclined towards it than her. "I worry that this places you in danger still."

"But it must be done," came the soft reply as she put a hand over his, making his skin burn with a sudden, wonderful heat. "It is the only way for you to be safe."

"And for our future to be secure," he agreed, closing his eyes briefly. "Very well. If you think it can be done, then let us do so. The engagement ball will be at my townhouse and I will hire additional servants for the evening. I have no doubt that Chiddick will choose one less loyal to my house so therefore, I will make my expectations for them all quite clear."

"Very well." Lord Wrexham put one hand on Andrew's shoulder for a moment. "You have my support."

"I thank you."

"Look." Miss Grifford squeezed Andrew's hand. "Lord Chiddick is approaching."

A knot tied itself in Andrew's throat but he forced himself to smile and turn to his cousin who greeted them all amicably.

"A very pleasant ball, is it not?" he asked, turning to Miss Grifford while Andrew's frame immediately grew tense. "And are you to dance this evening?"

"Oh, I had not thought!" Miss Grifford laughed and then took her dance card from her wrist, though she handed it to Andrew first. "Forgive me, Lord Chiddick. I must give this to my betrothed first, though he will give it to you thereafter."

Andrew watched his cousin out of the corner of his eye, seeing the way Lord Chiddick's smile seemed to freeze to his face. There was no happy glint in his eye now, no joyous smile spreading right across his face. Instead, it was as though every ounce of happiness had been torn from him and he was forcing himself to appear joyous instead. It gave him an almost statue-like appearance.

"Betrothed?"

Andrew nodded as his cousin's eyes swiveled towards him. "Yes, that is just so."

"You are engaged to Miss Grifford?" Lord Chiddick rubbed one hand over his chin as though he were forcing his expression to change from the current one it had frozen in. "Goodness, that was... unexpected."

"But wonderful, is it not?" Miss Grifford said cheerfully, making Lord Chiddick nod fervently – a little *too* fervently, Andrew thought to himself.

"Of course. Of course! Very wonderful. More than delightful," came the reply. "I am sorry I did not know already for otherwise I would have asked for a round of congratulations from everyone here."

"Ah, but I have not forgotten you, cousin," Andrew said quickly, hoping to placate his cousin a little. "I was just about to come and tell you but also to beg of you to keep this news to yourself for the moment."

Lord Chiddick lifted an eyebrow but said nothing.

"I am to throw an engagement ball in ten days' time," Andrew continued, quickly. "That shall be the moment I make the announcement. The *ton* will not know of my engagement until then. Might I beg of you to keep your silence for the moment?"

Lord Chiddick smiled briefly though Andrew did not much like the shard of steel in his gaze. "But of course, cousin," he said, firmly. "I can certainly keep such news to myself. Thank you for considering me trustworthy in this, cousin."

Andrew smiled while, at the same time, curling one hand into a fist – a hand which he kept behind his back for fear that his cousin would realize his true response. "But of course, Chiddick. You will be invited to the ball, of course. I do hope you will attend. It is important to me to have family there."

"I shall certainly be there." His cousin smiled and then held out his hand for the dance card. "Might I take a dance with your betrothed, then?"

Forgetting that he had Miss Grifford's dance card in his hand, it took Andrew a moment to realize what his cousin meant. Seeing it, he quickly put his own initials down for the waltz and the cotillion, before handing it to Lord Chiddick. "But of course."

"Wonderful news," Lord Chiddick murmured, looking down at the dance card. "Capital. Splendid. Truly splendid." With a smile, he handed the dance card back to Miss Grifford and then took Miss Renfrew's before turning to take his leave.

"Let me fetch you all a drink," he said, putting a hand to Andrew's shoulder. "This is a call for celebration!"

Before Andrew could find an excuse, a way to say no, his cousin was gone, leaving him to look around the small, gathered group, catching fear in Miss Grifford's eyes.

"I will not drink it," he promised, as she swallowed tightly and nodded. "I know better than that." Taking her hand, he pressed it lightly. "You will not lose me."

She smiled at him then, relief in her expression as she nodded. "I trust you. Let us pray that all will turn out just as we hope."

Chapter Twenty-One

"Do not expect *me* to congratulate you."

Rachel pulled her gloves a little higher and did her best to ignore her sister, offering her only a small smile when she came to stand in front of her. They were just about to enter the Duke's townhouse and were waiting for their mother and father to enter before them. Rachel's stomach was already a little tense, aware that this was the moment that everyone in the *ton* would be looking at her, waiting for her reaction as they heard news about her engagement to the Duke.

Bettina was not making things any easier for Rachel and she was doing her best to ignore all the whispered words that came from her sister.

"Just know that every smile will be forced, every word will be a pretense and every nod of agreement will be false."

"Bettina, I do not care." Finding herself a little exasperated, Rachel lifted her head and looked straight back at her sister. "Do you understand? I do not care." Rather than feeling intimidated, rather than feeling frustrated and upset, Rachel found herself shrugging, her mind caught up with a good many other things rather than her sister's discontent over Rachel's engagement. "I have very little interest in your opinion on my engagement."

"You can pretend all you like but I know very well that you care what I think," came the harsh reply, though Bettina kept her voice low, clearly a little concerned that their father would overhear her. "Your Duke is nothing but a beast. He has nothing but discontent and anger in his expression *and*, no doubt, in his character. He has kept himself away from society, has pulled himself back from everyone in the *ton* and has chosen you for his bride, no doubt, simply because you will not be likely to complain at his discontent and melancholy. You are nothing but grateful for his consideration but I can promise you, your marriage will be nothing but pain and sorrow and you will come to regret marrying the Duke of Longford."

Rachel turned to her sister, grateful that the cool evening air was brushing against the heat in her cheeks. "Do not misunderstand me when I tell you that I do not care about your opinion, Bettina. I truly do not. I have no interest in what you have to say to me, I have no interest in your opinion of the Duke or of my acceptance of him. You may think of him in one way but I can assure you that you are wrong. *I* am glad that you are wrong for it means that you have no true understanding of the Duke's character whereas I certainly do. I do not care about whether you approve of it, whether you are truly delighted by it or whether you have any interest in it! I am happy to be marrying the Duke of Longford and I know that I will have a happy future with him, regardless of what you think."

Bettina said nothing. Her mouth opened and then closed again, her face rather pale as her shoulders dropped, seemingly a little stunned by all that Rachel had said. Without another word, Rachel followed after her parents as they made their way into the house, her head lifted and a smile on her face as she waited expectantly to meet the Duke of Longford.

She did not have to wait long. His smiling face was present at the door, one hand reaching out to her, though he made sure to greet her mother and father first. When her hand went into his, Rachel's heart swelled with the warmth of affection and she let out a long, slow breath, glad now to once more be in his company. What she had said to Bettina was quite true; she did not care about her sister's words or opinions. The only thing that mattered was the Duke himself.

"How glad I am to see you," he murmured, turning to put her hand on his arm. "Shall we all make our way inside? I have not yet to make the announcement but I shall, very soon."

She nodded, looking up at him as her mother and father both expressed their agreement. "Are you quite sure?"

He nodded. "Yes, of course. I have spoken to the staff at length and they are fully aware of what is expected. Should anything untoward occur, they are to go to speak to Lord Wrexham so that I will not be interrupted."

Understanding what he meant – and that he did not want to speak too openly in front of her parents, Rachel pressed her hand to his arm a little more heavily for a moment, seeing his smile flicker for a moment. Obviously, there was a great deal of concern about this evening and though he was putting on a jovial expression, Rachel could almost feel the ripple of tension in his frame.

"Lord Wrexham and Miss Renfrew are already present this evening," he told her quietly, as they came to the ballroom door. "Now, shall we enter?"

Rachel nodded, aware of how quickly her heart started hammering as they approached the door. The footmen opened it, Rachel glanced up at the Duke and then, they stepped inside.

The crowd and the hubbub which had been going on around them slowly began to quieten as every guest turned their attention to their host. Rachel snatched in quick breaths, swallowing hard as the Duke cleared his throat, ready to make the announcement.

"Good evening, ladies and gentlemen and thank you for attending this evening." The Duke turned his head to look at Rachel, smiling as he did so. "I should like to begin this evening with an announcement. I have recently proposed to Miss Rachel Grifford and, much to my delight, she has accepted and we shall soon marry."

There was not even a whisper as silence fell right across the room. Rachel had expected that someone would applaud, that someone might rush forward to congratulate them but instead, there was nothing but silence. It was as though every single person in the room was overcome with shock and surprise, staring back at Rachel and the Duke without saying a single word or making even the smallest noise.

Sweat broke out across her forehead. She did not know what to do. Should she just stand here and hope that, soon, someone would say something? Or ought she to fill the silence herself?

"My hearty congratulations!"

Looking around, Rachel caught Lord Chiddick stepping out of the crowd, a broad smile on his face as he began to applaud. This seemed to spark the rest of the crowd into action for they all began to clap along with him, with a few cheers and cries of delight coming thereafter. Rachel let out a slow breath and sent a grateful smile to Lord Chiddick, only to realize what it was she was doing. She was thanking the very gentleman who wanted to get rid of the Duke of Longford!

"Thank you, cousin." The Duke nodded in Lord Chiddick's direction though Rachel noticed how a muscle in his jaw tightened as he shook Lord Chiddick's hand. "Now, do excuse me. I must dance with my betrothed."

"How about I fetch you both some refreshment?" Lord Chiddick asked, his smile still on his face. "It would be my pleasure to lead this room in a toast to celebrate your engagement."

"How very kind," Rachel murmured, as the Duke began to lead her away, giving his cousin nothing more than a tiny nod. The music began and they began to dance, leaving Rachel with a lump in her throat rather than enjoying the dance in any way.

"We must hope this is it," the Duke murmured, softly. "We must hope that he will do as we expect and that our plan works."

"I am sure it will." Rachel was forced to step away from him during the dance, feeling her stomach tightening. Coming back to him, she grasped his hands tightly and looked up at him again. "But if he is to make a toast, how will we escape drinking whatever he procures for us?"

The Duke frowned, perhaps having never thought about such a thing as yet. "I – I suggest you do not swallow any," he said, slowly. "Though I will try and swap the glasses for us." He took in a deep breath and then released her again. "Have no fear, Rachel. All will be well. I assure you."

"A toast to the Duke of Longford and Miss Grifford!"

The cheer which went up from the crowd made Rachel's heart slam hard into her chest. Everyone around them was taking a sip of whatever they had in their glass but Rachel had not yet lifted the glass to her lips. She looked to the Duke, watching as he lifted the glass to his lips and tipped it up, though she noticed how it did not reach the edge of the glass. He had not drunk any. Copying him, Rachel caught Miss Renfrew's eye as she lowered the glass, fully aware that the reason for her friend's white face was because of the nearness of Lord Chiddick.

"Thank you, cousin." The Duke turned and set the glass back down on a tray held by a footman and Rachel, after a moment, did the same. For the moment, they were safe.

"Most considerate of you," Rachel added, managing to smile. "Now, Your Grace, shall we –"

"If you would prefer a brandy to the champagne, I can have something else brought to you?" Lord Chiddick gestured to the two full flutes of champagne. "It is *your* evening, after all, is it not?"

Rachel shook her head. "I would prefer to keep a clear head, but I thank you, Lord Chiddick. You truly are being exceedingly kind."

"But of course." Lord Chiddick looked to the Duke. "Cousin?"

The Duke shook his head. "No, I am doing as Miss Grifford is, for I think that is the wisest of situations. Though as she has done, I thank you for your consideration. It is very generous."

Lord Chiddick shrugged. "I want you to have the very best evening, cousin. After all, it is not every evening that one announces one's engagement!"

"Might you wish to dance, Miss Grifford?"

The kind voice of Lord Wrexham interrupted their conversation with Lord Chiddick and, with a nod of relief, Rachel stepped forward, more than willing to dance rather than linger in awkward conversation with Lord Chiddick.

"And I should dance with Miss Renfrew," the Duke said, following after Rachel and giving her a broad smile. "Excuse us, cousin."

"I thank you for your rescue," Rachel murmured, as they all approached the dance floor. "I presume no-one has come to you as yet?"

Lord Wrexham shook his head. "No, not as yet."

The Duke cleared his throat, leaning near to her. "I have every footman here aware that I will give them the equivalent of a year's salary should anyone come to ask them to do anything unusual. I have also made it clear that if they did not, if they choose to remain silent and consequences fall upon anyone within the ball, they will be removed from their employ without hesitation."

"And I have found my footman," Lord Wrexham told her, as they found their space on the floor. "All we need now is for Lord Chiddick to act."

"A glass of water for you and His Grace, my lady?"

With relief, Rachel reached out and took the glass from the footman, only for the footman to clear his throat and catch her attention. "Yes?"

The Duke reached out and took the other glass but the footman took a step closer, his eyes flaring – and in an instant, Rachel understood she ought not to take a sip.

"Andrew, wait!" she exclaimed, as the footman looked from one of them to the other. "What is it?" Directing her question to the footman, she saw him blink furiously.

"I believe I am being watched, Your Grace," he said, quietly. "You said not to make it obvious but might we speak?"

The Duke gave only the smallest nod. "Of course. Rachel, be sure not to drink." He looked to the footman. "Go about your business. I will be in the hall in a few minutes."

Rachel looked at the glass of water in her hand, noting how there was a slight cloudiness there that she would otherwise not have noticed. What was it that Lord Chiddick had placed in the water? Her whole body shuddered. Lord Chiddick was not only cruel enough to attempt to injure the Duke but had also tried to injure her – kill her, even!

"I should have called him out," the Duke muttered, his expression growing dark and reminding her of how he had looked when she had first met him. "If it is in both your water and mine, as I suspect, then – "

"We should walk," Rachel whispered, tugging him gently away. "If Lord Chiddick is watching, then we should not make it at all obvious that we know what he has done."

"Very well, but I must beg of you to stay near to your mother or your father while I speak to the footman."

"But you will come back for me?"

The Duke nodded, looking down and then, lifting her hand, pressing a kiss to it. "Of course I shall." There was a softness in his voice, a quietness there which spoke of a tenderness which Rachel clung to. "But I must keep you safe."

"Very well." Wishing that she was bold enough to push herself into his arms, Rachel let out a small sigh and then smiled. "But do return to me quickly. I will miss your presence even for a short while."

"As will I." Releasing her hand, the Duke directed her back into the direction of her parents and then, after a few moments, stepped away.

Epilogue

"You will confirm that it was Lord Chiddick?"

The footman nodded. "I have the vial also."

Andrew's eyebrows lifted, shock wrapping around him. "You do?"

Again, the footman nodded but pulled it out of his pocket, handing it to Andrew. "It says nothing but that is what I was given."

Andrew inspected it, taking in the small brown bottle and seeing no interesting or distinguishing markings on it only for him to smile. "That is excellent. I will need to speak to Miss Renfrew but I am sure this can be used to convict him all the more." Seeing the footman look away, clearly a little concerned, Andrew put out one hand and set it on the man's shoulder. "You have done well and will be given the reward I promised. All that is required of you is a little more courage."

"Yes, of course, Your Grace," the footman replied, looking back at him. "Thank you."

"You have it?"

A voice over his shoulder made Andrew turn, his hand dropping from the footman's shoulder. "Lord Wrexham. Yes, I have the footman here and he has confirmed all. I even have the vial."

Lord Wrexham nodded, his eyes a little round as he looked to the vial which Andrew held out to him. "Goodness."

"And you have the other footman? The one who served me the Queen's Cakes?"

Lord Wrexham nodded. "I do. He is waiting in the servants kitchen."

"Then go and fetch him but wait by the door until we call for you," Andrew instructed the first footman, who nodded and then stepped away. Looking back to Lord Wrexham, he gave his friend a small shake of his head. "It is at an end. I am displeased that I have to do this at the engagement ball but it must be done if I am to be protected – and if I am to protect Miss Grifford also."

"Of course." Lord Wrexham gestured to the door. "Are you ready?"

Andrew nodded, filling his lungs with air and then lifting his chin. "I am."

The door opened and Andrew walked into the room, seeing the many faces turning towards him. Most had smiles, some were frowning as though still taken aback by his announcement of an engagement though Andrew paid very little attention to them all. Instead, he walked to the fireplace, turned and then, after a moment, held his hands high in the air. "I should like to make an announcement."

The orchestra, who had already been prepared for this, did not lift their bows to their instruments but instead, set them down and vacated the room. Slowly but surely, those in the room all turned towards him and, little by little, began to quieten. Andrew caught sight of Miss Grifford as she came to stand by the edge of the crowd, her mother, father and Miss Renfrew near to them. Lord Chiddick, he noticed, as at the other side, opposite Andrew's betrothed, which Andrew considered something of a relief.

"I should, first of all, like to thank you all for attending," Andrew began, wondering exactly how he was to phrase this. "Unfortunately, it has come to my attention recently that there has been someone attempting to injure me of late... and another attempt was made this evening."

Lord Wrexham caught his eye, giving him a small nod as he came to stand near to Lord Chiddick, though Lord Chiddick did not see him.

"There have been three attempts now to poison me," Andrew said clearly, eliciting a few gasps from the listening crowd. "I have been saved from it, thankfully. First I received a warning from an anonymous source – though I still do not know who that was – and thereafter, my betrothed and then my friend saved me from certain disaster. I became more and more convinced that there was something going on, that someone *was* attempting to injure me – to kill me, even! And what made it a good deal worse was that my father, who passed away some years ago, died due to a deliberate act."

There came another round of gasps and Andrew waited for that to pass, aware of his hands curling into fists as he attempted to keep a hold of his own emotions. Talking about this was more difficult than he had anticipated.

"I will not go further into this, I will not express any details, only to tell you that I have discovered the culprit. I tell you all of this tonight so that you might be aware of the truth and so you might all protect yourselves from this ogre."

"Who is it?"

Andrew turned to see Lord Carmichael taking a step closer, one hand on Miss Grifford's shoulder, clearly not only concerned for her but also for Andrew himself.

"Let me explain," he said, turning his attention now to Lord Wrexham who still stood near to Lord Chiddick. "This person not only caused the accident which killed my father but also placed poison in my drink and my food – and then paid footmen to take those specific items to me. I have one of the footmen from the previous attempt present and my own footman from this evening, who has told me exactly what happened and what has taken place. It is to my great relief that my servants are loyal to me for without that, not only myself but Miss Grifford would have been gravely injured, for the poison – the poison in *this* vial – would have killed us both."

Another gasp ripped around the room as Andrew held up the small vial. Ladies clapped their hands to their mouths, gentlemen turned to one another in shock... and Andrew let his gaze turn to his cousin.

"I have the two footmen here, cousin," he said clearly, as Lord Wrexham clapped his hands and the two footmen stepped into the room. "They will both attest to what you have done. You paid them. You did something dreadful and paid them for their task though, I believe, they did not know what they were doing."

"Wait a moment!" Lord Carmichael put one hand to his forehead, his eyes rounding. "You mean to say that it is Lord Chiddick who has done such a thing?"

Andrew kept his gaze trained on his cousin, seeing how the gentleman had gone very pale indeed. The man swayed and then turned, but Lord Wrexham was there in a moment, his hand gripping Lord Chiddick's arm.

"It was your daughter, Lord Carmichael, who discovered the truth," he said, clearly, so that almost every eye turned to Miss Grifford. "She saw Lord Chiddick enter the apothecary and sent Miss Renfrew in to see what he purchased."

"And it was poison for rats," Miss Renfrew interjected, her voice carrying across the room. "And I saw him with that vial."

Murmurs and ripples of unease ran across the room as Andrew turned back to his cousin. Lord Chiddick had now gone very red in the face and his eyes were wide and staring, though his gaze was fixed to Andrew.

"You are the heir to the Dukedom, are you not?" Andrew spoke quietly, though he was sure that almost everyone in the room was straining to hear him. "You are not contented with being a Marquess. Instead, you wanted to take on the Dukedom as well, *that* is why you killed my father and then sought to kill me. Is that not so, cousin?"

Silence fell across the room. It was the quietest that Andrew had ever heard a ball become and it was solely because of everything that was being revealed in this one moment.

He swallowed thickly, waiting for his cousin to say something, to *do* something, whether that was to either flee from him or admit to what he had done.

Lord Chiddick dropped his head.

"You did not think you would be discovered, did you," Andrew added, when no-one spoke. "But I have a friend who warned me of your intentions. Whoever that was set me on the path of watchfulness and for that, I shall always be grateful."

Lord Chiddick lifted his head, his lip curling. "That butler," he spat, making a few people draw back from him such was the vehemence in his voice. "That ridiculous, foolish butler whom I threw from my employ before I departed from London. He was always prying over my intentions and – "

"And he saved my life, as did Lord Wrexham and Miss Grifford. Therefore, I shall find him and make certain that he is secure in his finances for life," Andrew interjected, speaking over his cousin though his very heart trembled at the dark fury in his cousin's voice. "I should have called you out over this, cousin. I should have called you to a duel but I did not trust you. I did not trust that you would not find a way to take my life from me through trickery and deceit so that you might achieve your goal."

"And you thought to try and take the life of my daughter too?" Lord Carmichael stepped out from the crowd, pointing one shaking hand at Lord Chiddick. "Simply because she is engaged to the Duke?"

Lord Chiddick shrugged both shoulders, turning him into a character which Andrew had never before seen.

"I did not know which glass she would take and which the Duke would take," he said simply and slowly, as though he were speaking to a child and attempting to explain himself in plain terms. "It was not about her. It was about him."

The shriek which went up did not come from Lord Carmichael, however, but from Lady Carmichael. She rushed across the room and began to hit Lord Chiddick about the head with her face and her fists, though Lord Carmichael quickly pulled her back. Lord Chiddick attempted to stagger back and to escape, but Lord Wrexham held him fast – as well as the fact that he was now surrounded by both gentlemen and ladies of the *ton* who were all glaring at him with clear and unmistakable disgust.

"Cousin."

His voice reverberated and even those who were beginning to shout at Lord Chiddick quietened, leaving him to look straight at his cousin with a calm, steadiness in his heart and in his mind.

"We are no longer family," he said, as Lord Chiddick looked back at him, his lip curved into a sneer. "Should you dare to come near to me or to my betrothed again, I will not hesitate. Your life will be the consequence. I believe that I have shown you great consideration in this and that has not come because of my own desire. I have come to care for Miss Grifford and knowing what sorrow and pain would be left should I have demanded a duel was enough to hold my hand back. But I shall not do so again."

"And you have my support!" cried Lord Wrexham, beginning to march towards the door, pulling Lord Chiddick with him. "Out, Lord Chiddick! Out from this place – and out from society!"

The cry did not take long to go up around the room. Almost every person present began to sweep towards Lord Chiddick, forcing him towards the door. Andrew caught sight of his cousin's mouth opening and closing as he shouted some things – things that Andrew could not hear – but it was with relief that he watched his cousin be pulled to the door of the ballroom and swept out from it. Turning, he walked towards the two footmen, who both looked very pale indeed.

"Your Grace, I did not know about the cakes."

Before Andrew could speak, the footman dropped his head, his shoulders rounding though his words came tumbling out.

"I was asked only to bring them to you and to you alone. I did not know there was anything in them. My guilt has been so great that I have hardly slept but I swear to you, it was not purposeful."

"I believe you." Andrew waited until the footman lifted his head though he saw how the man would not look at him. "You bear no disgrace and I shall make sure that you are not thrown from your employment. You are both dismissed for the evening – and I shall reward you both for your honesty and your courage in this." Smiling, he set one hand to the shoulder of his own footman. "Send the orchestra back in. The ball must now continue."

"Your Grace?"

Swinging around, Andrew opened his arms and Miss Grifford rushed into them. It was not entirely proper for a gentleman to be holding a lady so close but Andrew did not care. This was what he needed and he prayed that she felt it too. Relief poured into him as he held her tight, his eyes squeezing closed as he felt her shake just a little.

"It is over," he said quietly, pulling back just a little and looking down into her face. "It is at an end."

"It is." Trembling still, she managed a smile as she looked up into his face. "Is Lord Chiddick gone?"

Andrew nodded, then pulled her gently to the quiet corner of the room, the shadows wrapping over them both and hiding them from view. Most of the gentlemen and ladies were still chasing Lord Chiddick away – though he might well be in his carriage by now – and Lord and Lady Carmichael were speaking fervently together across the room. For the moment, they were quite alone.

"Are you quite all right? That was a difficult moment." Searching her face, Andrew lifted one hand and pressed it to her cheek, seeing her eyes close as she let out a slow breath. "I am sorry it has been so difficult. I did not ever expect it to be my cousin."

"It is I who should be asking you whether or not you are quite all right," came the quiet reply, her eyes opening as she took a small step closer to him, her hand settling against his heart which immediately began to pound furiously. "As you said, this was your cousin and that must have been a great shock to you."

Andrew smiled briefly. "It was. But I am relieved to know that the threat is over. He will not dare to come near me, either here in public or at the estate. I do believe he was arrogant enough to think that he would never be discovered."

Miss Grifford's eyes searched his. "Are you contented now?"

"Contented?"

She pressed her lips together and looked away, her hand falling back to her side and Andrew felt the loss of it immediately. "This engagement... our marriage, it was never meant to be. I know we have spoken of it and you have expressed your contentment but now that the truth about your cousin has been discovered, now that it has been made known, I must wonder if you are truly as contented as you have said." Her eyes caught his again and he saw the worry there. "I do not want you to marry me unless it is something you *truly* desire, even now."

Before Andrew could stop himself, he had dropped his head and, in that moment, pressed his mouth to hers.

It brought with it such a myriad of sensations, he could not quite contain himself. His arms went about her waist and he pulled her close to himself, feeling her hands press lightly against his shoulders – but not to push him away. Instead, they slipped around his neck as the kiss deepened.

It was all quite extraordinary and wonderful in its own way. His chest tightened as his heart began to sing, a realization beginning to sink into his very soul.

Then he broke the kiss.

"I am contented," he breathed, softly. "I am more than contented, Rachel. It is in this moment, in this realisation that we are free from my cousin and free from all fear and concern that I finally accept what it is within my heart." Swallowing hard, he took another breath and then spoke what he had finally realized about himself. "I think I am in love with you."

Her eyes flared wide. "What?"

"I love you," he continued, finding his lips curving into a smile as joy began to bubble up within him. "It is not only an admiration of your courage, of your kindness and your devotion and nor is it a mere appreciation of your beauty and your character but it is a *love* which I do not think I have ever felt before. I cannot imagine being apart from you. Our marriage is something that I yearn for, something that my heart aches for because not only will we become husband and wife, we will step out into a future that is bound for happiness rather than merely putting up with one another. I do not expect you to respond to me in any way, Rachel, for that is not at all what I am demanding. All I am expressing to you is what I have finally realised I now feel... and that is that I have fallen in love with you." Laughing softly, he shook his head, running one hand over his eyes. "When I first came to London, I was determined to be apart from society, to stand back from everyone and keep my own counsel. I did not even *want* to be here, I did not want to spend time with others and it was only Lord Wrexham's encouragements that brought me to London. I was in a dark and shadowy place, garnering for myself a beastly reputation, being rude to you and to others and thinking only of myself. I was quite determined that I should never think about courtship or the like, only to now find myself in quite the opposite situation!" Smiling down at her, he lifted both hands to her face, tenderness welling up within him. "It is because of you, Rachel. This is all because of you. You have brought me a new freedom, a new happiness, a new joy and a new heart. I find myself in love with you and that has brought me so much, I do not think I shall ever be able to repay you... though I shall try, every day of my life."

Miss Grifford blinked and it took Andrew a moment to realize that she was crying. His heart slammed hard into his chest and his smile faded, making him quickly drop his hands. He had said too much, had expressed a great deal and how she had been overwhelmed by it – and just how foolish he felt himself to be!

"My apologies," he said, quickly, making to step back. "I should not have said so much and – "

"I am not crying because I have found it too much, Andrew!" Miss Grifford stepped closer to him again, her hands at his arms so that he could not move away from her. "Do you not see that I am crying out of sheer joy?"

Andrew's heart lifted again. "Joy?"

"Yes, my love! Joy!" Laughing quietly, she pulled herself closer to him, so that his hands wrapped around her waist again. "I have fought strange feelings towards you for some time, have berated myself for them and told myself that I ought not to have any such feelings for you! Indeed, even when you proposed courtship, the reason that I wanted to consider it was because I was afraid of what it would do to my heart."

"Your heart?"

She nodded, still smiling softly. "My heart is yours, Andrew," she said, softly. "It has been yours for some time, I think, though I, like you, was not entirely certain as to what exactly it was I felt. However, I find myself in love with you just as you are in love with me – and what happiness it is now to be able to tell you of it!" She laughed again as a tear dropped to her cheek. "And what overwhelming joy it is to know that you return my feelings."

Andrew dropped his head and kissed her again, his happiness greater than he had ever imagined, his heart almost singing for the sheer joy of this moment. Here he was at his engagement ball, free from any fear, any concern and any uncertainty and now looking to the future with the only expectation in his heart to be one of happiness.

"I can hardly wait for our wedding day," he whispered against her lips, her fingers brushing through his hair and sending heat racing right down his frame. "I cannot wait to make my vows and become your husband. I swear to you that I shall spend every day of our marriage doing all that I can to show you just how much you have become to me, how much I value you."

"And I cannot wait to become your wife," she whispered, her eyes fluttering closed as she leaned into him again. "I love you, Andrew."

With a small, contented sigh, Andrew bent his head and kissed her again. "And I love you, Rachel," he murmured, "with all of my heart."

The End